By the same author

Frames of Mind
Heights of Folly

Courting Trouble

by

Philippa Bunting

The Pine Marten Press

First published in 2015

© Philippa Bunting 2015

ISBN 978-0-9933493-0-0

Typeset and cover design by GSB (Edinburgh)

For Beatrice and Beki

Chapter 1

She sat in a corner diametrically opposite his own. She was reading
'Vanity Fair.' He gradually made this out, for want of anything
better to do, watching for glimpses of the title. Personal items were
spread like a stockade around her. It was surprising she could read
at all, the way the train swayed and lurched.

They were the sole occupants of the compartment.

Hugo yawned. A minute later the girl yawned too – yawns
being triggered by hunger, boredom, nervousness and fatigue. Or
suggestion? Perhaps she'd noticed his yawn. He wasn't inclined
to be flattered by young women catching up on their scholastic
reading.

Trust James to suggest meeting at the crematorium tomorrow.
Discretion was the watchword enjoined by his friend in the United
States Embassy. Yet the manner in which James himself behaved?
High profile farce.

Tall. Light blue eyes, very straight above wide cheek bones.
Long hair. Teeth remarkably even, shown to advantage during the
yawn. She was messing about with them now, nails tapping on
the enamel, rubbing at a front one. In his mind Hugo invented a
pretext for speaking to Vanity Fair. Something about the position
of the window? Conversation might flow for the remainder of the
journey.

'Would you object if I put the window down? It's quite close in
here.' He gestured urbanely.

She lifted a shoulder. 'No, that's all right.' She averted her face.

He sat back, closed his eyes and slept.

An abysmal din of echoes and slamming. Hugo staggered to
his feet, put on the jacket of his pale, tropical suit, and flicked
the lapels. Then tactfully he helped his companion open the
recalcitrant train door. 'It seems to have jammed,' she told him
with apologetic irony.

Fresh from Thackeray's voluptuous intrigues, how could she have coped better? 'Don't forget your book,' he ventured. She had put it down for the struggle.

'Oh. Thank you.' Brief smile. He followed her at a leisurely pace to the barrier. Here she glanced at him and said goodbye. No smile this time. She moved towards the taxi rank where he too was heading.

'Are you being met, or queuing?'

She replied she was being met – and retreated another pace.

Free of ticket and obligations, Hugo relaxed. But where were those Brighton taxis? Vanity Fair was hanging about still. He turned to her. To Becky Sharp? To Amelia Sedley? With which heroine she had identified? – and asked for whom she was waiting.

For her mother.

Well well. No – he wasn't waiting for anyone. He had a flat in Kemp Town which he used as a bolt hole from London. His mother's actually. Rather a sad visit on this occasion, being the anniversary of her death. And where, he asked his companion, did she live?

What a catechism of questions! But chance was a fine thing . . .

Fulking? That sounded familiar. A village below the Downs. Her name was Octavia. Unusual. The Eighth child, presumably? No, no, not at all, only the second actually. Shared laughter at Mother's fine disregard for pedantry.

'And whereabouts in Fulking?'

'Phlox Cottage. Not right in the middle.'

'I see.' Pause. Commit that one to memory. Come on taxis. 'Probably as well your mother doesn't have seven other children to organize.' A worse pause. 'Have you been to London for the day?' He now saw that her eyes were speckled.

'I don't know London very well. I was there for a job interview and wandered around a bit afterwards.'

'And where did your wandering take you?' Patronising oaf! He inwardly winced, while she cast about in her mind for an impressive lie. He must be forty at least!

'Just getting the feel of it.' Watching people, window shopping, sauntering in Trafalgar Square with all the tourists. Not setting foot anywhere as challenging as the National Gallery. Well, let him think what he liked. She was a serious reader if he'd only noticed –

which of course he wouldn't have. Octavia was struck by his grey eyes, elegantly clear. He was a large man but his voice was gentle. A sort of Good Samaritan on the radio voice. 'I've a brother who lives in London. He works in a tea company.'

Mrs Ransome floated up. Octavia bungled the introduction. 'Sorry, what's your name?'

'Hugo Talbot,' he told them. 'How do you do?'

'Roweena Ransome. Are you a friend of my daughter? How jolly.'

Mrs Ransome grasped his hand and gave it a slow, calm shake. 'A pick-up, actually. We met on the train.'

Mrs Ransome vigorously blew her nose. 'Wicked of me to be late. I got held up. Makes one so hot.' She sprayed herself unconcernedly with Eau-de-Cologne.

'Your daughter kindly kept me company while I waited in vain for a taxi. Here come several now.'

'Perhaps we may meet again one day, Mr Halbuck,' Roweena said cordially, now the need to offer a lift was removed. 'One never knows!' She took her daughter's arm. 'Well darling. Did the Foreign Office like you?'

Octavia was gratified to see his eyebrows rise. 'I think so. I really enjoyed myself. They've accepted me, subject to the usual checks. I was warned it might take two months, although they expect it to be less.' She and her mother began to walk away. Octavia half glanced back. 'Goodbye then,' she bid him curtly.

He raised a hand in salute, with a small abstracted smile, and hurried to a taxi.

Octavia kept up with her mother's long strides. Roweena took her arm. 'That is good news, my pet.'

'Yes. It was really no problem. All the same, I'm absolutely fagged. Where have you left the car? Pray it hasn't been towed away.'

'I'm not a complete fool,' her mother replied equably. 'I didn't bring it into the forecourt. Wretched car, I sometimes wish an earnest constable would do away with it. How lovely about the Foreign Office, dear.'

There was a policeman. He greeted them politely, notebook open.

Five minutes later he watched them depart. Roweena was only marginally chastened. Wearing an ill-treated felt hat with a silver dog pinned in front, she handled the Morris Minor as though parodying a driver. She was really very attached to her car, admiring its vagaries and likening them to those of a nineteen-twenties sports car. She was the sort of woman for whom even a child's scooter might develop mechanical trouble. Her driving was of a piece, seriously reckless.

Octavia sat beside her as though immune, which she could never be; but too preoccupied to react.

Chapter 2

Hugo parked his Sunbeam Rapier and nipped into a florist shop to buy his bunch of flowers. Freesias. He usually bought freesias; his mother had loved them particularly. Then back into the car and away up to the crematorium.

He walked through the main entrance gates and began a casual perambulation. A south-facing slope, admirably well tended. As a present and potential customer he might do well to congratulate the Council on maintaining these high standards.

Just nice time to visit the Garden of Remembrance before James turned up. It was absolutely typical of James to insist on the Crematorium for their meeting, seizing on Hugo's attempt to put him off as the best reason for going ahead. Would he be suitably inconspicuous? Fawn raincoat – or slacks and anorak? Not likely! For this absurdly incognito occasion, James would be rigged out in his best Savile Row suit. He would be sporting a Liberty's silk handkerchief, a bowler hat even – and a tell-tale, button-down shirt! The all-American Englishman.

'Hugo, my dear fellow. Did you take me for a piece of statuary?' James Wedge emerged from behind a marble construction, looking as if he and it were perfectly in period. He wore a linen sun hat at a jaunty angle; and there was a carnation fixed to his blazer. He refrained from shaking hands or making an overt display of friendship. The American accent was a further contradiction to the contrived English image.

'James! Punctual as ever.' Hugo continued his deliberate progress towards the small plaque he had had erected in memory of his parents. There, he bent over and set down the freesias. James was a good ten minutes early, a standard secret service technique which Hugo should have anticipated. Then he would have been able to greet his interred family first, before that other business. He placed the flowers where he always left them, thinking lovingly of his parents, letting James wait.

'Don't let me chivvy you.' James was examining roses growing nearby. Seeing Hugo turn away, he came over. They both surveyed the hushed, park-like precincts, remote from housing and commerce.

'Let me say at once that the evaluation of your mission has been very positive. I'm delighted. I consider it a direct tribute to myself, of course. Your written report was brilliant.'

'Did you enjoy my Laotian proverb?'

'Very much. A word in your ear, though. Don't overdo the erudite humour. State love it of course. But our clients in the Pentagon . . .'

'Indeed. The simpler American verities.'

'Quite. Bless your perspicacity, dear boy. A quality so often lacking in the intelligence services, so-called. Now, brace yourself. Our clients are sufficiently impressed to be considering a follow-up. Don't suppose I need tell you why Xiengkhouang is of such interest just now.'

'And I don't suppose I need tell you why it's so dangerous! I rather thought I was through with Xiengkhouang.'

'Dangerous? Or impossible?'

"Oh, it's possible. In some ways I'd quite like to go back. Get a bit more material for my book.'

Hugo watched a hearse rolling up to the memorial chapel. Other cars were approaching. He was back in a sombre theatre of death, with secret witnesses. James's choice of rendezvous revealed a psychological insight after all.

'But why Xiengkhouang again?' He saw James widen his eyes, as though anticipating that light must dawn. 'All right, don't tell me. I can guess.'

James seated himself on a granite curb. He placed his hand on a marble book, spread open and draped with ivy, his finger tracing one of the white, weather-stained ivy leaves. 'Merely to make contact again. A simple, straight-forward exercise in grass roots communication. You being supremely suitable as someone the Meo trust. The follow-up needn't involve you.'

Hugo wondered how many tons of ashes had been scattered in the Memorial Garden over the years. Witnesses, but essentially mute. Infinitely discreet. 'Very well. I don't know that I altogether approve. But I'll do it.'

James cupped a paternal hand round the buttocks of a small cherub reclining on the open book under the benign gaze of an angel – a cherub seemingly intent on cracking the mystery of reading. 'Strange to say, even here in this affecting place, your co-operation is a pleasure, Hugo. You do the morale good.'

Noticing dark stains on the angel's wings, Hugo made a mental note to ask the Council to get the sculpted marble cleaned. James went on, 'The mission will, as I say, be perfectly straight-forward. This time you walk in with the American anthropologists whom you met in Vientiane. After settling them, you walk out again. The rest will be up to them.'

'You mean the rest will be up to the White Star Teams. I know the scenario. All quite clear.' Perfectly clear; and if not perfectly safe, at least not all that dangerous. Not immediately. If word got round that Hugo Talbot was helping to infiltrate American counter-insurgency units, it would be goodbye to any further work among the montagnards for him.

'Anything we need to discuss as regards money?' James rose to his feet. He glanced down at the protective curb as if expecting to find it dented, patting his pockets.

'No. Not at this point. In the longer term, it's the publication of the book which matters to me, as you know.' Hugo held out his hand to receive the brown envelope James had produced. He transferred it into his own pocket. They started to retrace their steps towards the gates. No one else had been near them.

'I'll need the usual receipt for that.'

'Of course. Come back to the flat? Or are you afraid we'll be trailed?'

James gave a wry smile. 'You seem to forget, Hugo. The spider at the centre of the web must replenish its larder. Doesn't it occur to you that I drove down with more on my agenda than a moment of bliss in the crematorium? Delightful though that was. I've a round of commitments.'

'Not involving the new university, I hope?'

'Do I detect a whiff of snobbishness? But why do you suppose any such thing?'

'Because the crematorium happens to be on the way there. And because our own first meeting took place in the groves of academe. Spies are so predictable, James.'

James nodded his head slowly several times, hiding the ghost of a smile. Hugo went on, 'You'll be giving your presentation on the Two China Policy, I expect?'

'I'll be giving a perfectly standard talk on United States policy in the Pacific. To what I hope will be a hand-picked group. Provoke some polemics and make myself available for individual discussion later. Perhaps I'll ginger things up with one or two historical parallels. The Southern Sung, for example.'

'Is your seminar open to the public?'

'No.'

'But, as a distinguished academic, I could get in?'

'I'd regard it as an unfriendly act if you tried.' James consulted his watch. 'A less hostile act would be to invite me to your flat next weekend. I'd like to have more time in your company, dear boy, in more relaxed circumstances. I feel I've been tactless, thrusting practicalities into your annual pilgrimage. But I thought you might need the money.'

Hugo sat in the Rapier after James had driven away, quietly reflecting. He observed himself in the mirror. A well-shaped head. Hair quite long for an older man. Inclined to curl at the neck, the curlier bits turning grey. His eyes met the eyes in the mirror with an expression of, I wonder?

Chapter 3

James's arrival at Kemp Town was punctual to the minute. He presented Hugo with a paper bag of fresh Danish pastries, and at once began nosing about, making himself at home.

The place was just as Hugo's mother had left it. James liked his friends to establish personalities for themselves. Hugo's personality, in its Kemp Town manifestation, was too perfunctory. The oddments from his collection of tribal weaving suggested something extraordinary; but none was displayed to particular advantage. Not even the grand piece, hanging over the fireplace. And where was the evidence of a bookish colleague? No library shelves stuffed with volumes on South East Asia. Just a very modest array. As for the worthy oak antiques mixed with Ercol furniture! James looked round, concealing a smirk. There were framed photos of Hugo's parents and a studio portrait of a strikingly handsome young woman. Visiting the lavatory, he stuck his head into the two bedrooms. No change. He also opened a door he hadn't tried before. It turned out to be a large airing cupboard.

'I do wish you'd buy yourself another jersey, Hugo,' he remarked, his brief tour completed. 'That brownish one doesn't do you justice. See that you get one for Christmas. An indulgent aunt, perhaps?'

Hugo, good-natured ever, expressed himself ready to receive a jersey at any time from James himself. He was sure his friend's taste would make him the envy of Mayfair.

James was still prowling round the room as if on an assignment. He paused by the studio photo. 'Who is this lovely lady? Yes yes – your mother in her youth, you say. But you don't take after her. Sons ought to look like their mothers. I certainly did.' Standing back from the window, he subjected the front street to professional scrutiny. Then he joined Hugo in the kitchen and repeated the procedure, with the modest garden and its glimpse of the sea as the object of his attention.

Hugo was preparing coffee in a careless, English way. 'Find a plate for your pastries. In the cupboard up there,' he said. He enjoyed watching James cope in the kitchen.

They sat in the dining end of a large Regency room, with high ceiling and bold cornice. Hugo invited James to help himself to one of the three pastries. He intended to have the extra one. James needed to lose weight.

'There's a canopy bed in the Portobello Road,' James announced as he took the most succulent pastry. 'I've set my heart on it. It is my bed. It just remains for me to find the money. As a matter of fact,' he admitted, eyes narrowing, 'it's to be delivered in a couple of days.'

'James the First's bed at Knowle,' murmured Hugo. 'Now there's a four poster for you.' Then looking startled, 'You've bought it?'

James nodded. 'Alas, yes. You'll be filled with envy.' His face took on a soft shrewdness that Hugo knew well. 'What are the rest of our plans for the day? I can't emphasise enough how agreeable it is having civilized collaboration in one's work. Just think – your family might have come from Sheffield. I wouldn't be contemplating a weekend there.'

'My cutlery comes from there I daresay. Which reminds me: they're doing 'The Way of the World' at the Theatre Royal next week. Will you come, if I get tickets?'

James debated. Was Hugo growing casual? Jaunts to the theatre now. After all the pains he took to avoid the blatant, the unguarded. 'Very well,' he said. 'But find one or two other people. Possibly less conspicuous in a group. I take it I'm invited to spend the night?'

'I'll ask those Fulking people I mentioned. See if they want to come.'

'Good heavens Hugo! I don't want an introduction to them! Leave well alone; that's my advice. Now, what about this morning?'

'We could quiz antiques in the Lanes.'

James placidly drank coffee and mopped his mouth with silk. 'Oh no – much better not. Far too tempting.' He regarded his host with sinister reserve.

Hugo considered. 'What about a drive up on the Dyke,

10

prospecting golf courses? I've a fancy to take up golf with you. An investment against old age.' Reading James's expression, he added, 'Well, perhaps we should go to Fulking and have lunch in the pub. These little English villages nestling under the Downs are charming. We could take in Poynings parish church. There's something very satisfying and masculine about Poynings.'

'I'll be glad to have lunch and inspect the church.' James stood up. 'No golf. Now or ever.'

There was a public telephone outside the church at Poynings. Hugo searched in a local directory. Then, without making a call, he walked back to the Rapier and they drove on to Fulking. There, beside the Shepherd and Dog, a natural spring gushed from the rocks. Over it was a biblical quotation, set in tiles:

'He sendeth springs into the valleys that run among the hills. Oh that men would give thanks unto the Lord for his goodness.'

Beneath these heartening words appeared a municipal postscript:

'Not drinking water.'

Smiling, James nodded his head. He said quietly, 'Very true of life, in my experience. Nothing is quite as it seems.'

They went into the old English pub and ordered cordon bleu steaks and French fries.

Chapter 4

It was a radiant June day. Hugo had spent the morning combining an extensive walk over the Downs with another chance to see the Saxon church tower at Sompting. When he got back to the car he realised there was time for a detour to Steyning. According to Pevsner the nave of the church there was not just any late Norman nave.

Driving without haste, and spending approximately fifteen minutes at the church, Hugo found himself at the Shepherd and Dog well before one. He ate a ploughman's lunch with beer, sitting outside. He thought about his lunch with James, and about his impending Xiengkhouang mission.

The trouble with James's pleasantries was that they had a way of concealing unpleasant truths. Hugo had always assumed, as far as the Vietnam war was concerned, that the only conceivable interest of the Meo was as a rudimentary intelligence screen. The main conclusion of his own report was that there was no evidence of North Vietnamese infiltration in the border country. The old French airstrip which he had been asked to check was bristling with sharpened bamboo stakes as a deterrent to possible American parachutists. So much for the logistic infrastructure which the communists were supposed to be building up.

In which case, why go to the trouble of putting in White Star teams? And why let his own flair for winning the confidence of simple tribesmen be exploited? For the money? For his book? Or was it because, by keeping in with the Americans, he might hope to influence them? Rural England was so peaceful, so reassuring, that Hugo decided this was his motive. It did him credit.

A more immediate question was how to plan his afternoon. He listened intently to the bird song. Presently a party of young people converged at the table next to his. They were speaking German with a sort of controlled passion, Hugo thought, like singers of Elizabethan songs.

He was tempted to fall into a light slumber. He could hear spring water flushing over stones beside the steeply curving road. He was tempted to order another half pint.

He was tempted.

He asked for the use of a telephone.

No answer.

He started to walk up the village street. Cars coming downhill drove much too fast. They ruined the atmosphere here as everywhere in England.

It was quite by chance, he felt, that he took a cart track which led not only to a farm but to Phlox Cottage.

A nice house. A perfect shambles of an English garden. He wandered back along the track. One of the farmer's herd moaned lugubriously. A car hooted, a head poked out at one side, hat askew, hair awry. With a greeting of 'Good day to you! Hello!' the car of character came straight at him.

Mrs Ransome climbed out. She waved. 'Why, it's Mr Halbuck!' She was privately thinking, that impossible man. How awful of him to be here suddenly, without warning. But she forced a smile of welcome, while Octavia remained inside the car.

Hugo was all modesty. He took Roweena's hand with a courteous diffidence which Octavia unsmilingly noted.

Roweena exclaimed, 'How exciting to find you here.' She flung an arm at the garden and urged him to walk round it, asking him to tea, pressing him to have coffee when reminded of the time. A pot of coffee in the glorious sunshine. It was wicked not to enjoy the weather. Unsociable she might be by nature, from day to day, absorbed in her garden. But hospitable she must appear, faced with an intruder from outside. After all, she'd been in the Services, a naval officer's wife, and travelled and done her duty across half the globe.

Hugo was taking in Phlox Cottage. It was built of brick, tile hung, deep roofed, and with handsome chimneys. On one side there was a bay window. Wisteria swarmed over the porch. Less than a mile way, the Downs began to rise. The garden seemed rampant. Superannuated hollyhocks, not staked out properly. Gladioli. Nasturtiums which, he was later to learn, reminded

13

Roweena of life in Durban. Trellised roses swaggered or tottered down the path to a lichen-clad cauldron containing unhappy water lilies.

Fruit trees. A rustic tennis court.

Hugo toured the garden. He was charmed by all he saw, swept into Roweena's world by the enthusiasm of her manner. He said, in quiet contrast, 'You'll think me most impertinent, looking you up. I just happened to be passing through from Steyning, and seeing Fulking reminded me of the other evening. You have a splendid herbal area here. How often does one see fennel growing? And two kinds of sage. And thyme!'

'Ah, thyme,' said Roweena.

'Do you cook with it? Delicious with lamb, I always think. Aromatic, with a tang of bitterness.'

'As a matter of fact, I never cook with thyme. An aggressive herb. It has antiseptic qualities, you know. It can suppress, as well as purify.'

Hugo allowed himself a smile, as if a pleasantry had been intended. Roweena continued, 'Cats are the culprits. Cats make a beeline for my herbs. They seem to bed down in them.' Hugo's smile became more cautious. 'Now lavender is different,' she went on. 'The great balancer. If you suffer, as I do, from migraines, you would appreciate the properties of lavender. It stimulates the auto-immune system of course, and positive thinking as well. Drop oil of lavender on your pillow at night and you'll sleep the sleep of the just. And keep mosquitoes off!' She stooped suddenly. 'Mint is a useful plant too – more like a weed really. You're welcome to some.' Her tulle scarf interfered with an attempt to gather it for him.

'Thanks very much. I'll put it in a potato salad.'

She straightened suspiciously, dusting her hands on the scarf before thrusting them into the pockets of her long, donkey-brown jacket. 'You're interested in gardens, Mr Halbuck?'

Inspired to kill two birds with one stone he said, 'Please call me Hugo. Talbot, by the way, not Halbuck. Hugo Talbot.'

'How very friendly.'

Roweena spoke as if she hadn't heard. 'Octavia!' Her daughter had been idly trailing them. 'Make some coffee. Bring it on to the lawn, would you kindly?'

Hugo protested feebly that this was adding insult to injury; but Roweena would have none of it. Still suffering from the rude shock of invasion, she was determined to be as taken with him as he was with the garden. They arranged chairs under the greengage tree. Octavia disappeared.

'And what do you do in life?' Roweena demanded.

This was the sort of question Hugo liked. Comfortably nonchalant rather than circumspect, he launched along a well worn path, explaining that he was on the staff of the School of Oriental and African Studies. The minority tribes of the former French Indochina were his speciality. He had laid the foundations for his 'modest reputation' with a book about the Kha of southern Laos, an ancient people, still living in the stone age. In northern Laos there was an overlay of more recent settlers; in fact the situation was changing all the time, as more and more hill people moved down to fill the vacuum caused by the Indochina war.

'Wonderful people,' he assured her. 'When you can win their trust.'

'And you travel in Indochina a good deal, I imagine?'

'Oh yes. I spend most of the year in the field. I need the facilities of the university when I write up my results. I spend the working week in London, but I keep the flat in Brighton as a welcome escape.'

'Now that is exactly the sort of life I would fancy, if circumstances were different!' Nursing one knee across the other, Roweena added, 'I suppose you have no tiresome family to tie you down?'

Hugo was admitting the truth of this when Octavia approached with a tray of coffee and biscuits. She declined to take a biscuit herself, and her mother quipped, 'As if she need worry. Look at us!'

Hugo was amused, secretly glad he'd resisted rhubarb crumble at the Shepherd and Dog. He took a biscuit to show Vanity Fair that risks were to be taken.

As soon as Roweena gulped down her coffee she excused herself and went into the house. She had to call her builder. Slates were coming off the roof.

Hugo, alone with the girl, fell back on questions – kindly, probing questions. He wished she hadn't tossed her hair so resignedly when he turned to her. Perhaps the builder wouldn't answer the phone ...

'What's your opinion of 'Vanity Fair'?"

'It's good. Less comical than Dickens. But pretty funny in parts.'

'Yes. A wonderful humour. Becky Sharp for example. Now there's a girl after my heart.'

Octavia dealt him a cool glance. 'I think she's selfish and shallow. At least Amelia is genuine.'

Ah. Hugo opened his mouth to counter, but was cut off. 'Becky Sharp is cleverly conceived – if you can believe in her. But would anyone be so consistently awful? She's at least three people. Amelia's more realistic.'

'Becky Sharp is magnificent. And I can assure you, it's perfectly possible to be at least three people. Blameless Amelias are quite unbelievable.'

Hugo smiled. She didn't. He, poor sucker, was dazzled by the vicious Miss Sharp – while youth bristled on the side of morality. He spared her the trouble of further analysis, just as she felt she was off.

So – what did she do with herself?

She explained. 'I've been accepted for secretarial work in the Foreign Office. Now I'm waiting while they check my credentials. It may take a long time. I'll have to find a temporary job meanwhile.'

'You're right to resign yourself to a long wait,' he said. 'Positive vetting is in the hands of the security services, as I expect you know. The world's greatest time wasters.'

There he was, still leaning over his knees, lavishing his attention on her. She was probably hating it. But his chair was insufferably narrow. It was simply the only way he could sit.

The mother rejoined them, overflowing with builder trouble: how they'd let her down and over-charged for skimped work; how she was almost compelled to admire their bare-faced cheek.

Abruptly, her attention swung back to Hugo. He found himself embarking on an account of the Royal Kingdom of Laos, 'land of the million elephants and the white parasol.' He omitted most of the political subtleties of his London dinner tables. He mentioned the Red Prince Souphanouvong. The Pink Prince Souvanna Phouma. The White Prince Prince Boun Oum. He described the

Buddhist soldiery's preference for shooting into the sky rather than taking life, and how in fertility festivals, the indiscriminate throwing of water in all directions took precedence over the firing of bullets. And all the time he was imagining Roweena with her wish come true, in a place like Vientiane, stringing for some newspaper – driving the Consulate demented – claiming amorous connections with all the Asian princes. No – that was a daydream too far.

Octavia was touched by his respect for it all. Desire stirred in her to go with the Foreign Office to places like Laos, a little country with three princes, a million elephants and a white parasol. Until that afternoon, she'd never heard of it.

Hugo talked on. 'A treasure ship?' repeated Roweena. Octavia regarded him steadily. She wouldn't urge him on. He intrigued her – but she wondered why he'd come, and when he'd go.

He eyed her too, lounging in apparent detachment. Or a cocoon of romance? Or more likely still, bored stiff with him? He fancied it might do Miss Sedley good to traipse around South East Asia in the humidity. He must keep his eyes averted. Concentrate on the madcap mother. Here he was, trotting out a scheme he hadn't mentioned even to James, simply to impress these women. 'It happened in the year of the French Colonial Exhibition. A boat laden with Laotian exhibits was waiting in Luang Prabang, the royal capital, to start the trip down river.'

The story unfolded of the sunken treasure. Hugo helped them visualize the temples in their scrupulously clean compound, each with its burnished Buddhas; incense; flowers real and artificial. He explained how the monsoon season had come and what apprehensive weather reports the patrol boat had given. He described the treacherous Mekong, 'seventh longest river in the world.'

His phrases lapped on, like ripples from the Mekong itself. Octavia dissected a dandelion. It was an odd impression that in addressing Mother, he was really tuned in to her.

The blind monk's warning. Roweena interrupted at once. Was this part of a mystical discipline? An Eastern clairvoyance, practiced among the monks?

The captain and crew's determination to embark on their journey, Hugo persisted. The terrible disaster which befell them in the rapids near Sayabouri. The loss of men's lives, of Buddhist relics, of jewels gold and silver. 'It was a pipe dream of mine,' he concluded, 'to promote another attempt to salvage the treasure under British auspices. Much of it was perishable of course: the silks and scrolls. But I keep mulling over a scheme to recover the rest and perhaps get the British Embassy to present them to the Laotian King.' He glanced at Octavia.

Roweena said, 'And the prophecy? I wonder if the spirits would approve.' She began to drag her chair round. 'It would be a gesture of goodwill from Britain, wouldn't it, at this difficult time? I'll tell you who could do it. Royal Navy frogmen.'

Octavia was suddenly smiling at him.

'Exactly my thought. Royal Navy frogmen.' What a smile! 'I may have to go to Laos and Thailand later this year. We have a role to play in Laos as Co-Chairmen of the Geneva Conference.' He managed to rise to his feet. 'Sitting here so pleasantly puts me in holiday mood,' he said. 'But because I have time at my disposal doesn't mean I can waste any more of yours.'

'Come again soon. Come and have a meal! But I expect you're one of those independent bachelors.' Roweena suspected he had friends everywhere and was accustomed to being spoiled. Yet he couldn't have been more grateful for a cup of coffee. She was mollified by his manner after the small effort he'd extorted from her. Halbuck. Where had she heard that name before? Possibly it was some celebrated family . . .

They escorted him to the gate. 'Have you walked from Brighton? We must take you in our brute.'

'My car's parked down the road. I hope we'll see each other again.' He walked away, knowing they were ready to wave.

Roweena said to Octavia, 'What a perfect day to meet someone new. He was quite impressed by my humdrum garden.' She was carried away by his sincerity and her pretences.

Octavia left the gates. With a sense of futility, she headed for the house.

Chapter 5

Roweena spent most of her time in the garden. Anyone watching her would have noticed the odd methods she employed. The haphazard removal of plants and their installation elsewhere. Her way of murmuring to herself as she pottered about. Her sudden intervals of upright meditation, her surroundings seemingly forgotten. There was no ruling scheme. The garden reflected all that was most genuine but frustrating in Roweena's nature.

She was a large woman. She usually wore woolen jackets, long skirts and archaic, rustic hats. The length of her legs gave her a certain ungainly elegance but her feet were spectacularly big. She was apt to be shy, yet those who found themselves dismayed by her autocratic voice were as readily won over by her unaffected flamboyance.

Octavia had been reading Byron, Shelley, the lives of Byron and Shelley and a concise analysis of the universe. She read the Sunday newspaper cover to cover.

'What are you going to do with yourself, dear?' Roweena asked. She was on her knees, darning a threadbare patch in one of the sitting room rugs. It was an oriental rug they had inherited from her parents-in-law. Dotty little figures and mystical beasts. Roweena cobbled away at the loose area with the sort of ad hoc panache with which the rug itself had been made.

'I might find a temporary job in London. Associated Pictures Incorporated, where Isabel works. The film industry and Soho sound promising.'

'Isabel from Madame's Study Home? Such an attractive girl. And what if that's no good? Have you thought of asking Mr Halbuck if he has any suggestions?' Roweena was trying to re-thread the needle, narrowing her eyes like an old camel, pulling her mouth down. 'He has his publishing connections. Then the university, you know – SOAS. He might be full of good ideas.'

There being no reaction, Roweena worked on in silence. 'Where will you live?' she then asked, 'if you go to London? We must start thinking about that.'

'You know perfectly well, Muth. I'll move in with Nicholas. There's plenty of room.'

'And what about his flat mate?'

'What about him?'

'He's a man, Octavia dear. I can trust you. But can you trust him?'

'He's an overgrown schoolboy, Muth. Nick's known him for years. Try not to be so old-fashioned.'

Roweena swung round. 'Did I tell you? Mrs Falanage saw three small girls standing on this rug yesterday. They were holding hands. Isn't that rather nice? I wonder if they helped make it when they were alive.' She tilted her head at an enigmatic angle. Octavia refused to be drawn. She and Nicholas disapproved of their mother's obsession with spiritualism. 'Poor dears, their little fingers must have ached.' Roweena stooped over again. 'I wonder how they . . . but I mustn't be morbid, as Nicholas would be saying.' The needle stabbed fiercely in and out. 'Pass me the scissors, there's a dear girl.'

Octavia stretched. 'I can't wait to start at the FO and be posted.' She gave her mother the scissors. 'But I shan't get abroad till I've done a stint in London – they insist on that. I'm grateful now for my secretarial course – boring though it seemed at the time.'

'Really darling? Well, after all we've heard about culture, I expect there'll be plenty of it if you travel. Your father would have approved. Travel broadens the mind, he always said.'

When Isabel rang a few days later, Octavia had news for her. 'That man again! The one I picked up on the train. He telephoned from Brighton, how were we, bla bla bla. Then he said he had four tickets for the Theatre Royal, a Restoration comedy. Muth and I are invited, and the fourth ticket is for somebody Wedge, a friend in the United States Embassy. Mr Wedge sounds rather an old poppet.'

Isabel was not impressed. She said, 'Steer clear of older men, sweetheart. It would be spanks over knees in no time.'

Spanked over Hugo Talbot's knees? Octavia shivered. 'Really Isabel. What a debauched idea!' There was a pause, during which

Octavia pictured Hugo's Olympian detachment and herself, a willing victim, being deliciously humiliated. She hurried on, 'I warned him Muth talks during plays, I thought it only fair. He was very cool. Said the Wedge person grinds his teeth! False teeth probably.'

On first receiving the invitation, Roweena had been bright with good intentions to have Hugo for a reciprocal lunch. But all too soon she reneged. 'How can we expect the poor man to eat here when we hardly know him? He'd be embarrassed. I've no idea what he likes. Men are fussy. He probably only eats things with oriental spices. There'd be some difficulty. No, I can't offer lunch. Not yet, anyway.'

But to her dismay, Hugo turned up shortly before twelve the very next day, the theatre outing still a week off. Roweena was in the middle of ripping weeds from the rockery and unwilling to be disturbed. Bridling, she rallied enough to call, 'Hello! Excuse me if I slog on. Once I stop I can't start again.' She didn't at all see why she should stop. Best loved guests were often ignored.

'But of course.' Weeds flew through the air and fell about his feet, and over the path and some in the wheelbarrow. Casually he said, 'Hello Octavia.' She had emerged from the summerhouse with a carelessness to match his own. He cleared his throat. 'I wondered if I could take you both out to lunch. The Shepherd and Dog? Or there are little places in Brighton. Indian, Chinese – what you will.'

Roweena thanked him warmly. Then No, she said slowly, no, it wasn't possible. The pity being, she'd promised to look at some business affairs with her son.

Nicholas, down from London for the weekend, chose that moment to appear. Hugo appraised a head of wavy fair hair, a fresh complexion with a small mole in the centre of one cheek. Taller than his sister. But solid.

'Hugo, this is my son Nicholas. He probably feels he knows you already, he's certainly heard your name mentioned. Nicholas, this is Mr Talbot, our new acquaintance.'

Octavia leaned against a cherry tree. Introductions were absurd. Names, names. Well, at least Muth had got his right; and she would call him Hugo now, if she called him anything.

Hugo said, addressing Nicholas, 'Shall I try to reserve another ticket for the Congreve next Saturday?'

But Nicholas wouldn't be free. He was joining a party of friends in Lewes.

They were all standing about. Roweena felt consternation rising. Must she now produce lunch after all, with only kippers on the menu? Why the blazes should she?

As though reading her mind, Hugo turned from talking to Nicholas. 'Would Octavia accept my offer for lunch?'

'Oh – thank you.' She spoke with mixed feelings. Lunch with him on her own. She'd bore him. He'd patronize her. He might even rape her! Anyone else's mother would say No.

Roweena was remarking, 'I'm glad you're taking Octavia off my hands. All her friends are in London now. I wish she'd get together with the girls from Paris. She went to Paris for three months, d'you know?' She stood up. 'Now why did I think of that funny little Madame? It can't be the weeds. Lily Falange is so interesting on thought association. Nicholas dear, shove the barrow a bit nearer, would you?'

Nicholas obliged, saying, 'Yes Tavia, that's why Muth sent you to Paris. To make smart friends.' His eyes indicated Hugo.

She laughed tersely. 'For you to start dating, you mean. Don't fret Nick, I've got plenty of brainy beautiful girls in mind.'

'Isabel, for example.'

He spoke with such gentle mockery that Octavia laughed again, more indulgently this time. She said, 'Yes, Isabel! She's told me all about the time you got her back to your flat, by the way.' Noting the uneasy expression on her brother's face, she added quickly, 'The least you can do is get Oliver Monk lined up for me.'

Roweena weeded serenely on, relieved that these exchanges remained good humoured. Young people were so touchy about friends of the opposite sex. It had never been like that when she was young. She wiped her forehead. 'It's grand sport to watch a woman at work,' she said.

Nicholas pulled out a handful of couch grass. 'What about that party, Tavia? You could get all your posh friends down. I haven't heard you mention it lately, and your birthday was weeks ago.'

Inspired by Hugo's presence, Octavia declared, 'I've been thinking. I'd rather go to Russia. There'll obviously be time to spare before we hear from the Foreign Office.'

Nicholas gave a crow of amusement. Roweena said, 'How more than odd. Only yesterday I had out my book of Russian icons. D'you know, Lily can look at an icon and sense its origins, and what kind of person painted it.'

Octavia's head swung as though attacked by an insect. Her point ignored completely by Muth, as usual. So much for her bombshell about Russia. Lily Falange again. What would Hugo think? She said, 'Nick, will Olly be at the party in Lewes next weekend? Or is he still on holiday?'

'No. He got back last week. I thought I told you. You never listen. It's Spain all the time with Olly now, he can't talk of anything else. I'd say he's got withdrawal symptoms.'

'I want to see him while he still has a sun tan.'

'He'll have it all right. He looks a proper Spanish gigolo. But he won't be at Lewes, so you aren't missing anything.'

Hugo moved a step away. 'Shall I fetch you both before the theatre on Saturday?' He was beginning to wonder if he could rely on Octavia to be there.

'On no account.' Roweena was startled at the idea of such pampering. She'd drive them in. Save him dragging back out after the show. Save them the predicament of asking him into the cottage so late.

'We'll meet in the foyer then, at quarter past seven. Meanwhile, Octavia . . .?'

She suddenly realized she must tidy herself. Oh for the golden Oliver Monk! Instead, it was lunch and heaven knew how much further time spent with this person called Hugo.

Her thoughts, though mocking, were pleasantly sensuous. She hurried indoors.

Chapter 6

Hugo drove at a leisurely pace in the Rapier. She sat demurely at his side, hands folded in her lap, breathing lightly as advised by Madame in Paris. He asked her to tell him about the finishing school to which Nicholas had made such tantalizing reference.

'It was an enormous waste of time, to be quite honest. The only bright spot was this girl Isabel who's become such a friend. There was a rule about speaking French all the time. A total fiasco.'

'So you didn't feel yourselves turning into young Parisiennes?'

'No chance. We were hopelessly over-protected. We went everywhere in a group – and what's more we were chaperoned. A laugh really when you consider it's the radical sixties. Isabel and I were immensely daring because we chatted up some boys at an outdoor skating rink in the Bois. Isabel took up smoking, too.'

'Are you telling me you had no sexual instruction? From an institution that was preparing you for life?'

Octavia gave him an incredulous glance. 'God no. I expect all our dictionaries had the word taken out. There were no nudes in the art books we were given, either.'

'I think that's a very proper approach for aspiring English blue stockings. Emotionally low-key. You were there for the French polish on life, not life itself – laid bare.' The Devil's Dyke was passing on their right. 'Describe Madame. I adore headmistresses.' He sensed that her smile was a touch pitying.

After a moment she said, 'I don't think you'd have adored Madame. But she knew about real life, if anyone did. She worked for the Resistance in the war.'

'Did she indeed? Now that is impressive. I love the French. They make such crashing mistakes, and will never admit it. Were you told much about La Resistance?'

'Hardly a thing. But she used to operate from that very place, in Rue Erlanger. Hiding people there, helping them away. She liked a bit of spirit in her girls actually, and had quite a soft spot for Isabel and me.'

'Astonishing,' Hugo said. 'What about girl crushes? Was it a hothouse of emotions?'

His questions struck Octavia as so old-fashioned she began to laugh. 'We were only there for six months, though it seemed six years at the time. And we were all the same age, more or less. Crushes are on older people. Isabel and I were pretty well inseparable – but she's boy mad. She's got my brother in her sights right now. What usually happens is she frightens them off, or she loses interest when they get too fond. There's always some drama.'

'It's often the quiet ones who are the best bet. So the experts say.'

After a pause she said cryptically, 'You're not an expert, then?'

It was a case of the mocker mocked.

They were coasting along the Pavilion gardens now. 'The last time I went into that epic folly was two springs ago. The lawn was studded with crocuses, mauve, white and golden. Come on, let's park and think about lunch.'

It was to be a Chinese restaurant in the Lanes. Hugo commented on the pictures as they walked through to their table and sat down. 'These cheap commercial scrolls and reproduction pictures all have their roots in a very ancient tradition.' He indicated over her head. 'That's very like one small scene on a fourth century hand scroll in the British Museum, for example. I think they call it 'The Admonitions of the Imperial Preceptress' . . . something of the sort. Octavia and Isabel in trouble at finishing school, in other words. And there –' he pointed again, 'a typical impression of mountains and clouds and vaporous atmospherics. Another popular theme.'

'I like the horses crossing a river.'

'Yes. Charming, aren't they? Such comical attitudes . . . yet entirely convincing. Calligraphy is another aspect of Chinese art, such as you see on that huge hanging scroll.'

Green tea arrived and was poured immediately, before it could conceivably have brewed. 'A party of people in Singapore or Bangkok enjoy waiting for food to come. There's no hurry, the anticipation's almost the best part of the occasion. That's the test of a good Chinese restaurant, by the way – and there aren't many in this country outside London. The food's cooked after you've ordered. Everything has to be fresh. This place does it very well, that's why I come here.'

He helped her through the menu, advising on choice. 'You know how to use chopsticks? Green tea is invariably drunk – I hope you like it – but there's a modern tendency to start with something alcoholic, beer or brandy. Look, while we're waiting I might as well show you how to use these.'

He demonstrated with the chopsticks. 'Keep the tips level. This is the best way for beginners: the lower one you try to keep firm, between your middle and fourth fingers. This one between your first and middle fingers you flex about, and use to gather up mouthfuls. That's right!'

Putting theory into practice was more difficult. Hugo laid his hand over hers to steer her movements. It had the effect of making her giggle, but she gave up cheating with a spoon.

'We won't have a sweet,' he said when the dishes were empty. 'You don't want one do you? We'll just finish our tea, and leave. Having sweets is a European perversion.'

Octavia had decided to have lychees and ice cream, but didn't demur. She sat listening to his stories of other restaurants in other countries, horizons retreating and prejudices fading. They drank final cups of tepid tea and, after wandering through the Lanes, turned their steps in the direction of the Pavilion. It was closed for renovation.

'Never mind. Another time,' Hugo said lightly.

He put her back in the car and began driving through Kemp Town. 'Isn't this where you live?' she asked.

'Yes, quite near. I'll have to take you there one day. But now I thought you might like me to show you something else.'

It promised to be a dull way out of Brighton, alley after alley of stereotyped small houses with demolition sites in between. Yet – as though she had doubted his magic – there appeared before them a splendid old house which, at second glance, seemed to be falling into decay. In all directions paved terraces had encroached, enhancing and insulting the mansion's grandeur.

Hugo pulled up at the gates on which Keep Out was printed. 'I expect you know about this place,' he remarked.

Octavia had never seen it in her life. Scrambling through the wooden gates, she confessed as much.

'Barry,' he told her, standing on the neglected gravel courtyard and staring at the front elevation. A loggia. Three arches over slender columns.

'Oh,' said Octavia. The Peter Pan one? No. Obviously not. She began to pace eagerly up and down the forecourt. It was like looking at a beautiful building for the first time.

A sullen pewter sky was gathering overhead. The house seemed to shrug off its misery with aristocratic phlegm, squaring itself against treacherous elements and immeasurable time. 'Come along, we'll just skirt round the garden before it rains,' Hugo suggested.

Octavia needed no urging. She set off almost at a canter, picking her way over fallen masonry and broken glass to the back. There were derelict statues and urns, and the wall to a sunken rose lawn was within a whisper of collapse. Two nymphs, with chipped faces and fingers, postured to each other from distant corners, scanty ribbons streaming like petrified pennants.

'It's lovely. But how sad.' Octavia paused for breath and gazed first at the house, then into Hugo's pink-tinged face. Her own cheeks were glowing with excitement in the unseasonable rawness of the afternoon.

'It is sad. Another heart-breaking example of waste and indecision. This house, you know, is similar to the Travellers Club. A little later, I believe.'

'Look at all the windows. Nearly every one smashed. Who did that? Why can't the Council do something to save it?' An idea sprang up: for her family and Hugo to join forces in the name of conservation, possibly buying the place. A sequel to the treasure boat saga.

'It's a sitting duck to the youngsters of the neighbourhood with nothing better to do. They sneak in, they toss a few stones – and what a gratifying amount of damage is done! It's shocking of the authorities to let a house of this significance fall apart.' His tone changed. 'Now I'll tell you what it means to me. This used to be a boys' preparatory school. I spent four years here.'

'Really Hugo? How amazing!' She reflected on this news. He watched her. 'Then there should be an old boys pressure group to fight for it. Headed by you.'

He looked almost coy. 'Perhaps all those old boys are as

philistine as anyone. But don't be too harsh. There may be a militant campaign being waged to save it.'

'But you said yourself, it happens all the time. Nobody does anything! It's inevitable.'

'My dear girl,' said Hugo – and he said it so nicely she felt pleased, not condescended to – 'My dear girl, this sort of situation isn't at all inevitable. Plenty of buildings are saved. Very often by those local communities you were so quick to condemn. If you feel strongly about this house, join the Brighton Civic Society. Take action. Involve Isabel. Involve Nicholas. It may bring them together.' Damn, he cautioned himself, I'm talking like a Dutch uncle.

She received this as a snub, he believing she'd do nothing. 'Was it fun at school here? Were you the naughtiest boy?'

'I was a little angel,' he said smugly.

'I don't think!' It was hard to imagine him a small boy, good or bad. She was secretly rather moved.

They found a way into the house and made a hasty survey. Under Hugo's influence, it was natural to notice the grace of the rooms, still with their cornices and mouldings. Hearing rain pattering on the roof, they looked up and watched as it dripped over the dirty boards at their feet. There were stains which showed where the weather had leaked in before. Hugo tried to recall the schoolrooms as he'd known them then. He wore a pensive expression.

'We'd better be off.' He let her lead the way to the front yard and the car. So she liked it!

'One day I'll take you to another house, still more dramatic. Much earlier. A kind of moated grange. But starker. A Sussex version of Emily Bronte.' Expounding on this property, which he'd in fact never seen, a sense of his own conceit touched him. He'd overdone it. Was he trying to impress her with architecture – or with himself? What if her pleasure was a pose? She'd think him an ineffable bore. Deflated, but continuing to talk as if she was a favourite pupil, Hugo drove slowly out of Brighton and over the Downs.

Chapter 7

They met outside the Theatre Royal at the weekend. Wearing a mauve satin dress with a hip sash, dilapidated buckle shoes and a floppy hat, Roweena reeked of scent. Hugo led her into the foyer and up to the bar leaving Octavia to follow.

They found James there. A luxurious oval face, black hair scrupulously parted. Cynical eyes. A pale grey suit with a pearl tie pin. Octavia studied him covertly. Hadn't Hugo called him a bit of a dandy? Hard to say how old. She didn't like his deprecating smile. But his American drawl was amusing. If only Nicky had come – he'd have great fun with Mr Wedge.

James bought them drinks, which Roweena received in her grand manner. Suddenly Hugo disappeared and returned with an elderly person whose tanned, lined face made him look like an ex naval man – and who turned out to be just that.

'Guy Beamish is someone I've known most of my life,' Hugo said.

'I'm an old friend of the Talbot family. Haven't any of my own, never married, used to be very fond of Hugo's mother. Such a dear charming lady she was. A ready wit, always fun, great company. I miss her terribly.'

Bells rang for the second time. 'Drink up, drink up. We must move,' James chivvied. To his slight dismay, Guy Beamish was occupying a seat in front of theirs. Even as the safety curtain rose, he and Roweena were swapping notes on Egypt during the war.

'The Way of the World' wound its exotically contrived course. The production had been cautiously praised by the critics. Hugo was glad the sheltered Miss Sedley was reacting positively. Roweena too was laughing outright, often when no one else did.

A safety curtain descended at the Interval on which a succession of advertisements flashed while someone played the piano. Hugo suggested taking Roweena to the bar for another drink, but she had removed her shoes. She explained the situation frankly and fanned herself with her hat. Her cheeks were a dull red. Guy Beamish lost no time in twisting in his seat and returning to Alexandria. 'No, I wasn't there during the war. Ship just looked in. Did you say your husband ran the shore facility?'

'As a matter of fact, since we can mention these things now, he was in Naval Intelligence. Hated it – or so he said, though actually he had a talent for it and you couldn't get anything confidential out of him. Like blood from a stone. Such a pity you weren't in Alex. Gilbert loved it, the Sailing Club, the harbor. We might so easily have coincided.'

Turning to Octavia, Hugo began a game of finding the letters of the alphabet in correct order from the printing on the screen. It was as much fun as any nonsense with her contemporaries. He was already at K when she grasped his arm and demanded 'Will two Cs count as a D?' and Hugo, capturing her hand between both of his, pronounced her defeated. Her head and her heart reeling, it dawned on Octavia that for all his extra years, Hugo seemed the personification of youth.

Only then did Hugo realize James had deserted them, driven off by their silliness. 'He'll be at the bar,' he said. 'Shall we go too?'

They went, not to the bar, but to explore the theatre. As they trespassed into hushed annexes, Hugo confided that he had considered writing a small book on provincial theatres, so rich they were in curiosity. Helping her through a doorway, he found it natural to take her hand again. He was leavened with a dark excitement and felt almost reluctant to return to their seats. James grunted sourly as he rose to let them pass, ducking his head and contemplating his hands until the curtain lifted.

I'm levitating, Octavia thought. I'm literally floating. Then her elation subsided as the play went on. She was struck by Guy Beamish's interest in her mother. She tried to see her as he did. She wondered about those shoes. Would her mother get them on again?

Hugo had booked a table at English's. He asked Guy to join them but the offer was declined. They trooped down Castle Square to East Street and occupied an upstairs table. 'Tell us what you thought of the Congreve, James,' Hugo said.

'Well, if I'm to be honest, I'd say it was a fussy production.

Fussy costumes with glaring anachronisms; too much business from Fainall and Mrs Marwood.'

'But Jenny Sendell?'

'Oh first rate,' said James warmly. 'The definitive Millamant. Quite delicious. 'I nauseate the country' – how wonderfully she brought that out. I always enjoy her acting. This promises to be one of her vintage roles and we're lucky to have been amongst the first to enjoy it. I'm grateful to you, Hugo.'

'I thought the costumes were hilarious,' Roweena enthused. 'Mrs Marwood's hat! It put mine right in the shade.' As she spoke some of its raffia trembled against her cheek and she removed it, laughing at a memory of her own.

Hugo silently disagreed with James over Jenny Sendell's acting. He'd found her loud and mannered, not his idea of Mrs Millament at all. His idea, he told Roweena, was that she should be not much more than a girl. 'She's a youthful idealist,' he murmured. 'That's the whole point. Half the wit is lost if there isn't a core of integrity. That's what I like: a mirror image world.'

James had been listening to this quiet exposition. 'Oh balls,' he snapped. 'That's quibbling.'

Hugo gave him a neutral glance. But James wouldn't be brought to heel. He sat unrepentant until their fish arrived.

'Balls,' Roweena muttered pensively. 'I don't know when I last heard a man use that expression. Not for years. Gilbert would never say it – even to his friends. I expect it's different in America.'

It was James's turn to glance at Hugo, as if repeating the word.

Soon afterwards the subject of Suez came up. James said, 'Seldom can such a political outrage have been committed through sheer blunder. As to Hungary, what did you expect?'

Roweena remarked, 'Never shall I forget being precipitated from Cairo to the Suez docks by a drunken taxi driver. On two wheels most of the way. Between deep dykes of water. I thought my last hour had come again and again.'

Octavia wished her mother would stop her monologue so that she could follow a new exchange between the men. 'I'm disappointed not to have seen the ghost tonight,' Roweena went on. 'Every first night the theatre manager appears and leans out from a box. I hoped I was sufficiently psychic.'

'You'd need to be super-psychic,' James drawled, 'since it

wasn't the first night.'

Roweena chuckled. 'Of course not. You told us what the critics had said. I am a duffer!'

Hugo warmed to her again. Her ability to laugh at herself was disarming.

James lit a cigar. 'You're interested in the paranormal, Mrs Ransome?'

'I'm fascinated. But I haven't the perceptions of a neighbour of mine. You'd be astonished at what she can tell you about yourself . . . and your nearest and dearest.'

'Apart from my being a skeptic, I doubt she could do much with me.' James puffed complacently, and the smoke drifted between them.

'Octavia may take to cigars in Russia,' Hugo joked.

James received the news of Octavia's Russian journey calmly. He permitted himself to advise her on three phrases in Russian. Then he glanced at his watch.

Hugo poured the last drops of wine and lifted his glass. 'Here's to unexpected friendships,' he offered.

Octavia was quick to seek his eye. But Hugo's eyes, as he drank, were on Roweena.

Chapter 8

Oliver Monk was a more sprawling young man than Octavia remembered, and decidedly no longer a schoolboy. His floppy hair and clumsy movements were engaging. But he was evasive. He sipped his sherry and rarely lifted his eyes from the ground except to look Nicholas in the face.

Her brother and his friend sat outside and discussed cars. Octavia listened with amused envy. Their self-absorption! She wanted to be included. At what precise moment would the intellectual tides turn and knowledge build, layer on layer? A fleeting image of young men at university took over. Eerily beautiful creatures, detached and breathlessly aristocratic. Exhilaratingly clever. Of quadrangles, ringing footsteps, ringing bells, soaring steeples and spring flowers.

Octavia's prerequisite of marriage was to share her early years with her husband. Breaking her arm in Mooi River; falling into rivers; near death on the seas in the Bay of Biscay. One doesn't live for nothing. Oliver wasn't quite right, but he was the next best thing. Now it seemed that her past had vanished suddenly. Watching her brother and his old school friend, she was eager to enter their present. They were still bandying jokes, intensely satisfying to themselves and inconsequential to her. She nibbled the rim of her glass, unaware of the dry smile with which she regarded them; and how much it unnerved their visitor.

Their subject was Spain. 'Think about it Nick.' Oliver set his glass on the ground to gesture his sincerity. 'You've got to believe me. Spain's the place for tourism. All you need is a bit of enterprise.'

'No cash up-front, of course?'

'Well yes – something to get you get started. But here's how it went for me: I go out there on a package holiday. After five days I can make myself understood. I sort out a couple of problems at the hotel – terrible place by the way. Before I know what, the local courier suggests I join the agency! She was quite a bird, really knew what she was doing. If we were out there with time to look around, we could get ourselves taken on, no problem. We could knock up a couple of little local guide books – this bird I'm telling you about reckons there's a mint to be made out of them.'

'Go ahead with her then.'

'No no. Don't worry, she's got her boyfriend, she doesn't need me. These couriers have a tremendous time. No, what we'd do would be to make money during the summer as couriers, then stay on for the rest of the year and write our guide books. Simple introductions as to what to see and do locally. I'm no good at that sort of thing but it would be right up your street. We could have the time of our lives. In the summer we could organize special expeditions into the interior, places tourists never visit. That's where I come in. We'd be a great team.'

'Rubbish Oliver! Return to earth. We'd be amateurs. As for the language, I can imagine you made yourself understood with the Spanish chicks! You didn't need the lingo for that.'

'Hey – come on. I sorted out a serious muddle at the hotel. Got several of our party into better rooms and managed to have the water supply switched on properly. The sort of thing I've a talent for. I've pretty well got the entrée to a tourist company in Barcelona. Small beer at first, but I spoke to a lot of blokes who'd gone to Spain on this basis. One of the lads has got engaged to a fantastic girl without a word of English! Well, one or two words ...'

Oliver's glance acknowledged Octavia's presence. She crossed her legs languidly. For a moment his eyes remained riveted on her.

'I'm sorry. I'm not convinced.' Nick folded his arms. 'One doesn't get oneself established in the City simply to chuck it all up.'

'But the City can wait!' Oliver stole another look at Octavia's legs, realized her smile was still upon him, and looked away. 'But to revert to cars – why don't you get mobile, Nick? Your life is sterile, man!'

'I don't need a car, living in London all week.'

'You could buy my little honey. She's done a mere forty-nine thousand miles. No vices I can remember. Can't think how I can contemplate parting with her. Fact is, I rather fancy taking Dad's

Land Rover off him. I'm going back to Spain, with or without you, and I'll take his old truck with me.'

Octavia listened to their talk, poised to cut in, to get Oliver to show her the 'little honey' which he'd tucked in against the hedge. It was white, fish-shaped, a sports car of exactly the sort he'd been advising Nicholas to avoid earlier in the afternoon.

Roweena appeared from the house. She cheerfully interrupted the dialogue with travel anecdotes of her own. 'And on that occasion, with twenty-four hours notice to evacuate, they unhinged the doors, put blocks of ice into my packing cases and, as if that wasn't enough, cook found himself arrested for theft. Wrongfully, as it transpired. I got him released from prison.'

The incredulity Oliver expressed seemed to apply as much to the narrator as to her story. He stood up to leave with an air of bemusement and lifted a hand at Octavia. 'I'll give you a ring,' he said, apparently seeing her for the first time.

Chapter 9

He telephoned some days later. Would she let him take her to a place he knew in the Lanes?

He handled his glamorous car with unnerving skill, reaching speeds that nearly stopped Octavia's heart. It was an MGA. He also spent a lot of time switching things on and off – the fan, the heater, the wipers – and gave inappropriate signals. She asked him if she could have a go.

'Better not,' he said. 'You wouldn't be insured. I'm not convinced I'm insured at the moment myself, if you want to know.'

'Just concentrate on the steering then,' she advised. 'Never mind the gadgets.'

He put out a large hand and pinched her knee. 'Naughty little busybody.'

His idea was to try a pub he'd recently discovered. They ought to patronize new enterprises.

They climbed a grubby stairway and sat overlooking a small square. There was an antique coin shop, a shop full of upmarket children's clothes and an alleyway with dustbins. 'Not exactly continental gaiety – but okay,' Oliver said. 'The food's supposed to be spectacularly bad, you'll be pleased to hear. What was the food like in Paris? You went out a lot I gather?'

Octavia vouchsafed the information that she'd found Paris faintly disappointing. There was a brief silence. One sentence for Paris – one thrust into the heart of France – and the subject lay dead. But Oliver was not unmoved. 'Really?' He gazed at her, eyelids drooping a little. 'Let me guess why: The nightclubs not up to much? Or let me see, wait for it – pregnant?'

She gave a burst of laughter. 'She wasn't that kind of Madame! Somewhere out there Paris was wicked and fabulous. But we were practically locked up. Blokes simply hadn't been invented. Such a sham.'

Oliver leaned over the table at her. 'How so, sham?' He was alert with interest. 'Was Madame really English? Or, perish the thought – a male in drag?'

Octavia pondered. 'She just wanted to believe that all her girls were paragons. In one of our last lessons she wrote in Isabel's loose-leaf Journal, 'Vous deviendrez grande artiste.' Can you believe it? You probably can, because you don't know Isabel.'

'I do know Isabel. Nick's friend, Isabel Gibbs. Madame probably meant a night club artiste.' He noticed the waitress. 'What'll you have? We'd like a couple of pints of Stella Artois to be getting on with.'

When they had ordered, Octavia said, 'I meant it about Madame. She liked her girls to be wealthy and talented. There was something stagey at the Study Home, come to think of it. Velvet curtains, which were always pulled across. We worked at a big table by electric light. There was a plush tasseled table cloth and lots of alabaster cupids dotted around. Why are men so interested in all this stuff?'

Oliver licked his lips. 'Cupids. What were the other girls like? I'm fearfully impressed by your little academy, Miss Ransome.' But what impressed him most was her dismissal of it all.

'There was a South American whose father was Ambassador in London. Probably still is. Another girl had a brother who's an equerry to the Queen.'

They drank their lager. During the course of the evening Oliver ordered a further pint for her and two more for himself. They ate only one course. It nevertheless seemed very late by the time he shook the chair he was on and scraped it back. 'Something the matter with the level of this floor. Typical sloppy conversion.' He became a touch lordly with the waitress. Leaning on his elbows, he said into Octavia's eyes, 'You haven't a lot of time for your native soil, I take it? Egypt, South Africa, France. Russia next. Are you a restless girl?'

He was handing her a ready-made glamour. Or mocking her. Too tipsy to decide, she shrugged. 'No. But I avoid ruts.' Something was beginning to annoy her, or she wouldn't have said that. She had nothing against ruts. In some moods she adored them. 'You seem very confident about working in Spain.'

'You bet. Of course, you're set fair for the Foreign Office. That's vastly superior as career prospects go. There's no comparison. But you don't ever feel you'll be tied to a desk? You wouldn't prefer the freedom I'll be enjoying – to up stakes and wander at will? No, I'm sure you wouldn't, and quite right too. You'll like all the posh partying and the grandees buzzing round for your favours.'

'I'll only be a sec-typist you know. And grandees don't interest me. In my experience, grandees are rather predictable people.'

'You're absolutely right.' Oliver stared glumly at the table. 'I can't see you bothering with grandees.'

He cast an inch of beer down his throat. Having choked and grumbled that the glasses were poorly designed, he seemed to notice her silence. She was getting tired. 'Sweet,' he murmured, cornering her hand on the rough table top. He pressed it. 'A memorable day in my life. A lovely, clever girl like you, a total stranger, looking at me with those limpid eyes. Letting me hold your hand. You really are sweet.'

Glancing at the clock over the bar, she was surprised to see that in fact it was still quite early.

They clattered down the stairs. 'Come back to my parents' place in Worthing. I can promise they won't be there.'

It sounded ominous. He cajoled, rubbing her elbow with his palm. 'Your mother will be disappointed in you if we're back too soon.'

The bungalow was in a street that led straight to the windy sea front. Oliver banged the doors of the MGA and fumbled for his house keys. In the sitting room he switched on lights, opened cupboards, adjusted a lamp and made manly bustle.

'Black coffee?' he called from a nether region. He brought coffee, declaring the need to clear his head before the drive to Fulking. He insisted they had a brandy. Octavia accepted in the spirit of adventure. She was blowed if she wouldn't discover a bit of sex for herself.

She drank half the brandy then strolled about. There was little to distract her. She picked up a clay sculpture, then quickly put it down: an unclothed figure touching its toes. What sort of people were the Monks, she wondered idly. She went to the window and peered into the dark night outside.

'Come and sit, Poppet,' wheedled Oliver, removing his jacket and sinking into the settee. Octavia felt hypnotized. She stifled her qualms and sank beside him.

'I enjoyed our dinner so much,' he said, snuggling his arm around her. He had brandy in his other hand. On the side table a lavishly refilled glass had materialized for her. 'You're a very sporting girl, a refreshing change. Isabel's told me such a lot about you.'

Octavia's mind raced. What had Isabel told him, the little snake? That she was refreshingly promiscuous? Before she'd worked out a strategy, Oliver pressed his lips against hers. She lay limp until he retreated, then sterilized her mouth with brandy. He lay across her and for a moment she wallowed under his atavistic urging, his hands groping her in wanton disregard. He tried to manipulate her hands on himself. At that moment she struggled free in a climax of frustration. It was no good. She was conditioned not to go through with it.

'Come and sit down, Poppet. Relax.'

'I think we'd better go. Please drive me back.'

Oliver staggered up, feeling for his brandy, nudging it over with his foot. He stumbled towards her. 'Poppet, I'm sorry. You're so nice. I was carried away.'

'Do carry me away,' she urged lightly.

The irony passed Oliver by. 'Good old Nick, eh darling?' he murmured, encircling her waist. 'I'll see such a lot of you now.'

Locking the front door, he took exaggeratedly deep breaths while telling her what a gentleman he was. In the MGA he became ostentatiously sober, driving them to Fulking with exasperating caution.

Nicholas welcomed them in. 'Have a nightcap Oliver?' He used hushed tones to suggest it was really too late. 'How drunk are you? Maybe you should call it a day.'

'I call it a great shame,' Oliver mumbled, a mood of self-pity coming over him. He raised a limp finger at Octavia, which she ignored. Then he went heavily back through the porch.

'Thanks again for a super evening,' she called after him. She watched as he noisily reversed. Eventually he had gone. She listened to the engine fading into silence, then returned indoors.

Nicholas was waiting. He gave her an enigmatic look and went back to his room.

Chapter 10

They assembled in the kitchen. Oliver's feet were bare and he had draped his discoloured socks over the Aga rail. 'I'm damn hungry. What about lending me a pair of socks, Nick?'

Nicholas went to fetch some. Isabel, huddling into her cardigan said, 'I think I'll have a bath, if nobody minds.' It had been her idea to play tennis, despite the wind and the need to dodge occasional showers. Nicholas had fallen over on the slippery grass in an attempt to shine. Isabel, spruce and vivid, had a triangular face with dark eyes and thick, crinkly hair.

'I mind,' said Nicholas. 'I'd like a bath myself.'

Isabel said, 'Me first.'

When she'd gone, Oliver shambled round the room doing a comic Charleston for Octavia's benefit, whistling 'Love is the Sweetest Thing.' His bare feet were unalluring and Octavia set about cutting slices of bread rather than behold them. 'I can't believe you're doing toast, the thought makes me so happy,' he said, supporting himself while he picked at a toenail. 'It's your mother's influence. You can read my mind.'

Duodenal rumbles sounded overhead. Isabel's bath was draining the tank.

They found Nicholas at the sitting room window, dangling a pair of khaki socks. Oliver held them up for inspection. 'These what you choose to wear? Not high in the glamour stakes, and bad for the feet. Feet need to breathe.' He sniffed the socks. Then he pulled up the piano stool and began to inch them on with finicky concentration.

Rain which had driven them in was by now exploding over the countryside. Luminous yellow, powdery grey, the light floated like dense water past the windows. Trees, grass, rose arbour – all was shrouded by falling torrents, gently menacing. Already the paths were awash.

Isabel appeared for tea only when the others had finished. She looked even more clean and shining than before. 'Ooh, the smell of hot buttered toast!'

'Just finished.' Oliver pushed himself off the sofa and wiped his fingers at the same time. 'Come outside Tav. The rain's stopping. We'll leave the love birds to wash up.'

They strolled through a sodden, potent-scented garden. A pair of thrushes bounced across the path in front of them.

'They've been well sheltered. They look dry, at any rate,' Octavia said.

Oliver licked buttery crumbs from his mouth and pressed her fingers to his lips. 'I expect Nick's told you, I'm going to Spain next week. Did he mention it? I'm selling the MG and 'buying' my father's Land Rover.'

'Are you really off? But Oliver, what's the long-term purpose? That scheme of yours for tourism?'

'More to dissipate my savings. Don't know how long I'll stay. A month probably. Maybe longer. A year, if things go well. I tried to persuade Nick to come and share the driving and funds. No go. He's getting a bit insular.'

'Will you be paid for going? I mean, are you being sponsored?'

'No, not at all. Pure escapism. But you'd be safe to bet I'll not quite lose touch. It has to be said, I'm fed up with working in London. No challenge. But you can believe me, Spain is inspirational! I quite fancy starting my own little business there actually, and it may well be tourism.'

'I'll miss you.' It was hard not to fill the role of lover. She sounded wistful. In this romantic setting she felt he expected it of her.

He hugged her. 'You're sweet, Poppet. I shall miss you too. But you'll find someone to replace me. Summer's a great time for a sexy girl. I must face up to that!'

She thought, Who says I need to find anyone? But she laughed ruefully. 'Men are impossible! One never knows where one is with them.'

He was delighted. That was entirely feminine and sporting of her. He led her to his car. He hung over the creamy field of its bonnet, gently wiping the rain away. 'It's when you wash a car you get to know its body, its details . . .'

He fondled Octavia's bottom as he passed round the boot.

Chapter 11

Roweena lay prostrate on her bed, a perfumed silk scarf over her face. She'd taken off her outer clothes and shoes. An antiquated fur coat was heaped over the chintz ottoman. Several drawers hung open. Photographs, magazines on the paranormal and hypnosis, potted plants, Turkish Delight, a shooting stick and underwear confused every surface. A sheepskin rug was rucked up beside the bed. There was a powerful sense of personality about the room. It was a friendly place.

There were good days and bad. Superstitious setting shoes straight, overprinting her handwriting, fearing fire and dreading death. The fear of madness. All since Gilbert died. Her sister had committed suicide with a shotgun in a field.

She's too lethargic to go into her own beloved garden! That's what people might have said, full of concern. But nobody cared. They were puzzled – or indifferent. Her children were merely used to her. The young were heartless. Now they were filling the house with their friends, every weekend.

That was what made it a particularly black day today. She could hear someone disrupting her bathroom. Voices shouting in the hall. Such careless high spirits. She moved the perfumed scarf on her face and it flooded her soul with dark, half-yearning thoughts of suffocation.

But these days passed. I must get a grip. I will rely just a little on this good man Hugo Talbot, Roweena told herself. He would be a staunch friend. He was a man of the world and had understanding. If he could only make sense of my world for me. At least no-one could guess what I go through. I hang on to convention, I entertain, I laugh and live like everyone else. When all the time it's quite impossible. I cannot mask my oddities to myself.

She remembered the happy days of early marriage when Gilbert had been proud of her willful nature. He was a great one for parties, even during the war. Especially then. Their bungalow in Cairo was famous. They'd been used to offering meals, baths, the freedom of the house to officers from all three services. She'd flogged herself up to each social hurdle and sailed over it with nonchalance. To land happy but drained on the other side. That was when she had servants, of course. It was different now.

Roweena's mind turned to her talks with Lily Falange. They got on well, they shared the sort of preoccupations other people were inclined to sneer at. Lily had second sight. Next time she saw Lily she would come out with it. She'd say, I simply want to know whether my husband was faithful to me. Not because I'm vindictive, you understand, just because I can't rest until I know. How would Lily reply? Why don't we have a Session, Mrs Ransome? I'm always ready to help. You know the Doctor and I like to do what we can . . .

It could never be. She'd be letting herself down. Lily seemed very discreet, as though she wouldn't say boo to a goose. Not an idle talker. But no. And yet – Roweena stirred uneasily – supposing she should die before she knew the truth? That would be more than she could bear.

The door opened.

Octavia noticed a rip in her mother's petticoat and a safety-pin holding it together.

'I know my darling,' Roweena said sighingly, folding the scarf. 'Remind me to mend it this evening. Have you had a lovely walk?'

'We played tennis. Then it rained.'

'Has it rained? How annoying.' She massaged her temples, still clutching the scarf. 'The scent of this does take me back to the Twenties! Your father gave it to me for motoring – I tied it round my head. I had such thick auburn hair in those days. I associate it with Egypt too. I know I wore it on some of our picnics.'

Octavia, sitting on the bed said, 'Oliver goes to Spain next week.'

Roweena swung her legs down, thumping the pillow. A faint hint of almond oil. 'Young men are restless creatures. We women have to be tolerant.' She gave a deep chuckle. 'The chances are, he'll stop in Spain. I should if I were a man, and I often wish I were. In my opinion, you deserve better.'

Octavia bristled. Perversely she said, 'How do you know I deserve someone better? Who said I wanted him anyway – or any man?'

'Quite right, darling. I don't expect you to have a man, as you call it. I never did till I was years older than you – and even then Gilbert upset me enormously.'

'What a testimonial for marriage!' Octavia had started tidying the room, heaping clothes together and picking things up from the floor.

Roweena, used to having all her remarks misconstrued, composedly dragged a comb through her hair. There was a photo of a small dog tucked into the mirror frame. 'Even now I miss my little Rufus. Do you remember Rufus, our wire-haired terrier?'

Octavia went over to her mother's cupboard and took down the brown beret with its silver dog brooch. It featured amongst her very earliest memories. She and Nicholas had always liked that brooch and thought it made their mother rather splendid. She said, 'We ought to have Hugo for lunch. We owe it to him.'

'Yes. We do.' Roweena spoke firmly but lay back on the bed again as if exhausted. 'We will give him lunch.'

'When?'

'Oh, when he's free. He's a busy man.' There was a pause. 'He must be rather bored with Mr Wedge. We'll have him to lunch and give him a break from Mr Wedge.'

'Will you ask him?'

'I'll ring him up. Remind me again, there's a dear girl. And tell me meanwhile what we should feed him on. It must be a light little lunch, nothing lavish. A baked beans sort of meal, with chops; that always goes down well with a man.'

'Not baked beans! We can't possibly give Hugo baked beans. He LIKES his food.'

'Then what?' Roweena demanded dramatically, already going into a flat spin as the occasion threatened. 'I used to think nothing of entertaining a dozen people at a moment's notice – and I fed them very handsomely, I can tell you. But I can't cook showy meals now. This is a simple cottage. If I invite him, he must expect simple food.'

'I'll plan a lunch,' Octavia promised, going abruptly to the door. 'And I'll cook it too.'

Oliver had said, 'I'm so fond of you.' Or had it been just, 'I shall miss you?'

Chapter 12

Nicholas sat on the dining room sofa, which sagged. He looked at a seed cake perched in the hatchway. All the birds of the air might have thrust their beaks into it, judging from its appearance. He stared glumly at shelves of naval books belonging to his father; at a musical box, a blunderbuss and an Egyptian horsehair fly swat.

Twenty to four. An afternoon wrecked by females. A nice fellow making a prize ass of himself for nearly one hour. But Nicholas wouldn't abdicate by walking out. He was still hoping to have a bit of rational conversation with Hugo himself. Nothing to do with tea business. Just a yen he had to go to South East Asia. His mistake had been in not taking Hugo off for a pint at the Shepherd and Dog.

His mother lounged in a chair with shabby chintz covers. The room was furnished in a combination of faded linen and dilapidated hide. Some dried mud clung to Roweena's stockings and a roll of garden string protruded from a pocket. She kept massaging her large hands. She had become rather cold, getting the dahlias properly spaced. These cool days were perfect for planting out. Never mind. She rose to fetch the cake.

Octavia had half ashamedly shown Hugo her pop song records. He'd called them a most comprehensive collection, and pretended to be familiar with the majority. Now, to Nicholas's dismay, they were quibbling over the lyrics. What exactly was Freddie Cannon saying in 'Fractured?' And Little Richard roaring out in 'Baby Face?' Was it this word, or was it actually that? As if it mattered! He made an obscene sound by strumming the pages of the telephone directory. Why not give Isabel a ring? Instead, he pushed a pile of newspapers aside and went to fetch teacups saying, 'Let's have the Stones, 'I can't get no Satisfaction.''

Octavia asked Hugo, 'Can you dance?'

Hugo considered her quizzically. 'And if I can't, would you

45

laugh at me?'

She began laughing. 'I might.'

'Well, I can.'

Roweena clapped her hands, long and hard to make them tingle. 'Let's see then! Let us see.'

The gramophone was crooning, 'Here comes Summer.' Hugo obeyed negligently, holding Octavia close with an air of detachment, as though mocking himself.

'Bravo!' cried Roweena. 'Bravo! Steady with that teapot, there's a dear fellow,' as Nicholas slopped some tea on the carpet. 'You must explain the niceties of this brand of leaf to Hugo. He's so interested in everything, and I can't always tell one from another. This lot was out of a gold pack.'

Hugo came to rest. 'Bravo she says. But I should like to see her dance, Octavia. I think we've made sufficient fools of ourselves for her amusement.'

Octavia was changing the record. Fools of themselves? But the 'we' pleased her. She picked up a Kinks record, 'All Day and All of the Night.'

'Something hot,' Hugo pressed. 'Give us a Charleston. Or the Black Bottom.'

'Oh now, wait a minute . . .'

'Nicholas,' Hugo ordered, 'support your mother in a Charleston.'

Octavia waited. Hugo's dancing had certainly not been hot. He'd moved her about in a quaintly sedate style.

Thinking himself pompous, Nicholas said, 'If my mother wants to do a solo, don't let me steal her thunder. I've a personal preference for mopping up tea, to be honest.' He left to find a cloth and Roweena, determined to be sporting, took the floor.

She began to caricature the music Octavia had chosen. With her large frame, her fluttering scarf and hands, her clumsy shoes, she was a touching spectacle. Octavia watched with affection, while Hugo gave vent to a long, low chortle that slowly gathered momentum. He went forward and put his arms around her. He held her close and they both jigged in unison. Nicholas, returning, averted his glance.

Almost at once, Roweena collapsed into the chintz chair. What a card, thought Hugo. He administered tea to her with such solicitude that Octavia wished she'd danced too, and had Hugo holding her close to him. But she laughed cheerfully, catching Nicholas's droll expression as he escaped upstairs. She picked out The Wonder Who's 'Don't Think Twice, it's Alright.'

Hugo said, 'Where's Nicholas? I'd like to talk to him.'

Roweena excused herself to finish hoeing. Hugo was tempted to go after her. He hung fire by the doorway, then caught sight of Octavia's face. Had he said something to offend her? A sulky disposition? Cautioned, he was still attracted. He reflected, This girl could be an albatross round your neck, Talbot.

Roweena was digging assiduously in the chalky soil when Hugo went outside. 'Isn't that a beautiful rose?' Octavia said, following at his heels and affectedly fingering its leaves against the wall. 'It's Madame Alfred Carriere.'

'Indeed it isn't,' her mother contradicted. 'It happens to be Sanders White. Aha. You've pricked your finger, I see. A little stinker for thorns, that rose.' Octavia grimaced. She knew she appeared ungracious. 'Best of children, will you kindly get out of my flower bed.' Stiffly, Octavia stepped aside. What a trial families were. If only she'd taken Hugo for one of her local walks. In Indochina and places he had to trek huge distances. They could have tackled the Devil's Dyke.

Roweena was saying, "'The Last Rose of Summer.' One of the tunes in our musical box. And 'The Prince of Wales.' How they take me back. Gilbert loved 'The Last Rose of Summer.'"

'They remind me of childhood,' said Hugo.

'You should go to Sissinghurst,' Roweena remarked. 'One of the best gardens in England. Not formal at all. Striking design and planting. It's open to the public now, you know.'

'I will,' Hugo promised. He watched her pressing in the plants and pouring water. He felt a positive admiration in his turn for the magnificent behind she presented. He'd seen her doubled over in this uninhibited way before.

'There must be ghosts galore at Sissinghurst. It was once a garrison for French prisoners. In the seventeenth century. The most atrocious conditions ever suffered by prisoners, we're told. In that heavenly place!'

'A grim contrast.'

'Ghosts,' went on Roweena, standing up. 'My garden's but

a poor thing, relatively speaking. But there's great serenity. The house is a happy house. I believe I'd know if troubled ghosts were here. But you'll think me a crank, Mr . . . I mean Hugo. Talking ghosts again. Heaven forbid they manifest themselves at our bidding. What truths they would tell! Nothing is as we see it.' She stared at him. 'Hugo. Such a special name. Lily Falange is good on names. I really intend to ask her round and introduce you. She's always busy. Very community spirited – unlike me. So quiet and modest you'd think. But she's the organising type.'

Octavia said sourly, 'Well, Hugo won't want her organising him.'

'Lily says those who have gone ahead are only too glad to help us mortals. In helping us they help themselves attain a higher sphere, you see. But the ways of the hereafter still remain a mystery. We can't deluge them with questions, poor dears.'

'Much better not,' Hugo murmured.

'Oh much.' Roweena hauled up a root. 'There are good spirits and bad, of course. Those that work for us and those that work against us. When we indulge our bad tempers, the evil influences cluster round us like flies over dung.' She confronted Hugo. 'Lily has actually seen an evil spirit, squatting on a drunk man's shoulder. Just like a monkey, she said. It doesn't do to have the wrong sort of people about one, certainly not for a serious Session.'

'How exceedingly alarming,' Hugo said. 'About the monkey.'

Nicholas approached warily. 'Mother, the crows have nested in the broken chimney again. If we don't do something about it the house will get riddled with dry rot. The air can't circulate.'

'Those elusive builders. One wonders how they keep in business. They never come, the wretches.'

'There are nests up in the loft above the garage,' Nicholas said. 'Swallows or house martins? I don't know. Come and enlighten me, Hugo.'

Hugo didn't hesitate. 'Rather. I was actually going to suggest a stroll into the village. Then I really must make tracks.'

They went to inspect the garage. Octavia watched them. Later, she saw them walking down the drive, their heads communicatively lowered. She knew what Nicky liked about Hugo's company: it was Hugo's way of mentioning places with alluring names. Just naturally, without a hint of conceit.

Saravanne. Phong Saly. The Plateau des Bolovens. The Plain of Jars.

She'd get to places such as these herself one day, if the Foreign Office would only hurry and complete her vetting.

Chapter 13

'Damn,' said Hugo.

'How so, damn?' James enquired.

'Just damn.' James, mercifully, hadn't overheard his telephone conversation. Those foolish women, he'd have said. Those time-wasting foolish women.

There wasn't so much time now. His field trip to Xiengkhouang was dictated by weather. He'd need to get there during the dry season, starting next month. His brief encounter with the Ransomes had surely come to a logical and graceful conclusion. Enough is as good as a feast, Hugo cautioned himself. But some tiny muscle stirred, and his stomach unfurled like a bird stretching its wings.

James was engaged for the following night. Hugo envisaged getting away to Sussex and taking Roweena somewhere. An exasperating woman, a travesty of a woman; but the sort of woman Hugo rather liked. He wanted to hear her talking about her wartime experiences. She never needed much persuading. Possibly about her marriage.

James's rooms in Albany were large and handsome. The somber purple carpet at Hugo's feet wasn't exactly attractive, but displayed James's collection of Chinese rugs to good effect. The curtains were of a carefully clashing maroon. The couch was maroon and at either side of a sturdy fireplace stood a leather chair. Two Chinese lacquer corner cupboards and a magnificent Chinese cabinet in ceiling-wax red gave crowning touches of splendor.

James sat engrossed at his desk. A straight-forward English nineteenth century desk but lit by a lamp covered in Chinese silk, the standard being a celadon green dragon. Hugo watched James at work. He wore a purple silk dressing gown bound with crimson braid. Modest CIA uniform indeed. And all this purple! James happened to be a card-carrying Republican.

As if aware of Hugo's attention, James glanced up. 'Join forces with me in Somerset this weekend. The Palmers. Regular house party. More pleasurable than useful in theory. But one never knows.'

'Sorry James. I can't manage it. I have to meet a chap at SOAS and spend some time in the library there, no doubt. Plenty to do in Brighton as well. Hours of writing and preparation.'

'Plenty to do in Brighton. I do hope that isn't a euphemism for doing the Ransomes. I think I shall coin a new phrase. Doing a Ransome – ie screwing up. They could become your Achilles' heel, Hugo. I kid you not.'

'Don't lose sleep over them. In a short while I shall be in Xiengkhouang, well beyond their reach. I'll be 'safe' as you so callously like to suppose. There's safety and safety, of course.'

Hugo, over a glass of whisky, gradually fell into an escapist reverie of Luang Prabang. He'd spent a few nights there with a missionary couple before his earlier expedition. They were a delightful pair and had an even more delightful pet golden gibbon. He saw a crowd of Meo tribes people approaching down a mud road, the women in their kilted skirts of black and red, black leggings and jackets, wide red sashes. Their tall black hats and, not least, those circles on circles of heavy silver necklaces. He could imagine Octavia wearing several of them. She had a graceful neck. He imagined her in Luang Prabang, discovering the Royal Palace and the temples; the steep, layered roofs. He saw her walking with the graceful hip movements of the Laotian girls, dressed in one of their long, shot-silk skirts. He found the Lao girls immensely appealing. It wasn't difficult to synthesise a well-do-do young Laotian with his taller, fairer Octavia . . .

As Hugo grew drowsy, he imagined himself discussing James's Jakata paintings with Roweena.

'Rather vulgar, some of them.'

Vulgar? He surely wouldn't say vulgar. Explicit. And Roweena says, 'I'm tired of Mr Wedge!' and takes his hands. But the hands grow smaller. It's Octavia after all. She's pleased to see James's secret world. She's inspired by her shyness to be bold. She marches right in to James's bedroom. She's staring at the bed. 'A four poster?' She's impressed. She thinks it very like the bed of a

Laotian prince.

Hugo sipped his whisky.

It made a pretext, of course, for whipping up emotion, for gripping her hard young arm with firm fingers. Like that!

Hugo shifted. He finished his drink. Stick to the Jakata paintings. Vessantara and Maddi on foot, carrying their children. I make her follow these stories in every smallest detail. She doesn't understand, I don't explain, but she's gratified beyond endurance; and beyond endurance are my sufferings as I feel her near. We don't hold hands. We're too intent on the pictures. The Brahmin binds Maddi's hands with jungle creeper, leading and whipping her on her way. She submits without a word, knowing this will fulfill her husband's greatest wish – to attain Enlightenment.

'Oh yes,' says Octavia. 'Oh yes . . . ?'

Chapter 14

The sun shone.

Hugo said, 'What a pity Nicholas won't come. I wanted to pierce his enigmatic front.'

'Oh really?' Octavia answered, deciding not to believe him.

They set off in the Rapier, driving to a spot where they could park, then departing through a valley on foot.

'I presume your curiosity is too great for words, since you haven't asked your usual questions,' Hugo said. 'Actually, I thought we'd look at a rather splendid house that Pevsner says is worth visiting. The one I told you about.'

She responded at once. 'I remember. The Bronte one!' She seemed to float along at his side with a bouncy cadence in her stride.

'It's called Park House. It's Jacobean, and it's privately owned.'

'Will we be able to see it properly?'

'In theory we won't. But in fact I intend to explore the garden and try to get into the house itself. I thought I might use you as the instrument by which I effect my entry.'

'What! Just barge in on private property? I certainly won't do that.'

'So your title of Naughtiest Girl in the School was fraudulent?' Aha – that needled her. He turned in time to see her chin lift. She was wearing what he was pleased to call her Bardot vest. Charming, but absurd for this kind of hike.

'Okay, fine. I'll march up to the front door and demand a sherry – and then lunch. If you don't dare.'

'Excellent.' Hugo smiled warily. 'But don't be alarmed when I flit into the trees while you thunder at the door. I shan't re-emerge unless you're well received.'

He consulted an Ordnance Survey map. Sure enough, a dilapidated stile seemed to confirm the existence of a public footpath. They set off.

'Now, let me tell you what Pevsner says. Sited at the end of a long lane, apparently part of the old drove road to Bolbrook. Excellent view to the south – which is unusual as a matter of fact. Front stone-faced, but if we can manage to get a glimpse of the sides they're half-timbered – or should be. Mullioned windows and interesting chimney stacks. Remember that please. We must spot the one that's star shaped.'

They'd reached the rim of the valley and were confronted by a barbed wire fence swarming with brambles. 'We'll never get through that,' Octavia said optimistically.

'Remember the Brontes.' Hugo forced two strands of wire apart. 'Nip lightly through. Beware nettles.'

She was through in a trice. He clambered after. They crossed a rough field, where Hugo had difficulty in making out the line of the footpath. 'All this detective work reminds me,' he said. 'I keep meaning to ask if you've informed the Foreign Office of your holiday to Russia?'

'No.'

'I know you're not officially employed yet, but they might take a rather dim view.'

They breasted another field which, according to Hugo's map, ought to have brought them to another road. A short way up to this, to the right, would be the drive to Park House. Their immediate problem was that the footpath was completely ploughed up.

'I don't want to seem interfering, but it might be tactful to drop the Foreign Office a line,' he added. The drive was there all right, he could see it already. He strode out with renewed confidence.

Blow the Foreign Office, Octavia told herself. As they turned into what appeared to be a private drive she began to drag her feet. 'Wait Hugo,' she said. 'Seriously. We're trespassing.'

'We're not trespassing. This is a public road. We've every right to go as far as the gate at the end.'

But at the end, with the merest glimpse of the house, it transpired that rights of way were not the whole story. 'The path veers off here, along the boundary hedge. But we're not to know that. We'll just probe the garden a short way. I'm determined to see the place, having come this far.' Hugo swung through the gate in a proprietary manner. 'Don't worry,' he assured her. 'The terrors of the law of trespass are greatly exaggerated.'

Ashamed of her nerves and his audacity in equal measure, Octavia followed, three paces behind. They passed between unkempt yew hedges and hurried down the grassy slope to a neglected tennis court. There were torn deck chairs and a rotting cane table. In a weary old summer house croquet mallets lay in an open box which resembled a child's plundered coffin.

'Come along wench.' Hugo flourished his stout stick over his shoulder, urging her on. She trotted after his retreating back until they came in full sight of the house down an elegant little lime walk.

Hugo stood rigid. The house was a ruin. A modern cedarwood bungalow had been erected close by.

'This is shattering . . .'

He looked totally disillusioned, the light in his eye faded, the tautness of his mouth almost tearful. 'But it's in Pevsner! It's a notable house. It's in Pevsner,' he repeated. 'What an absolute shame.' He stared in disbelief at the bungalow, silently drawing a parallel between vision and reality.

'I'm still glad we came,' Octavia said.

She'd think him ridiculous, especially after his bland homily at the Barry mansion. He lifted his hands. 'All right. Let's get the hell out of here before we're challenged.' He laid his bare arm heavily along her shoulders. 'We'll follow the footpath as far as Bolbrook. Perhaps there'll be a pub.'

On the way they rested under an oak tree enjoying a view of woods and hills. Shades of the ravaged house remained with them. Cautiously Hugo set out to recapture the romantic mood of the previous night. He started telling her about a diamond he'd been talked into buying in Singapore. It had been folly. He was inclined to think he should sell it, provided he could get his money back.

Nonchalantly, he brought out the diamond, casually wrapped in a handkerchief. He held it on his palm where it winked with liquid indolence. 'Hold it,' he urged her. She laughed as it glinted in the bright air. 'It's a blue-white,' he said. 'Very pure – like you.' She laughed again. 'I'm wondering whether to convert it as best I can. Or wait and use it one day. But it's too fine for a ring.' His eyes reflected the diamond's twinkle. 'Don't you agree? Doomed to be left on a wash-basin and lost for ever.'

'It would be a shame to sell it. It's so lovely.'

Hugo carefully rewrapped the diamond and slid it deep into his pocket again. They sat in silence. Octavia was conscious of having passed some sort of test. The sunshine had waned and a watery haze swept the sky. Suddenly Hugo laid her flat on her back and beat her with a rose he'd filched from the abandoned garden. The petals showered in her face, a thistle bit her elbow and she cried for mercy. Gazing down at her, he said, 'You look nice. A bit battered. Your eyes are a lovely colour.' A pause. 'I've been married already, you know. So I have a yardstick.'

Octavia never wavered. A greenish-blue light was focusing on his eyes, washing over his face, then lifing to pupil-point again. She said, 'Really?' and sat up.

'I was less cocksure in my marriage than I was in trespassing,' he replied. The stylish humility masked a flash of self-knowledge not unlike physical fear – an awareness of a cruel streak in his make-up which he usually kept well concealed. He thought, That was a stupid thing to do – the business of the diamond. It must be the coda to our little relationship; the graceful, the logical conclusion. I'll write an avuncular letter to her in Russia – and that will be the end.

He took out his map and spent some time consulting it without comment.

Octavia mentioned that she was seeing Oliver that evening.

Chapter 15

The Russian holiday approached. Hugo had promised to take Octavia out the night before she left. But at the eleventh hour he telephoned with a cold, calling it off. Anticipation turning to apprehension, she saw her Russian venture wear an increasingly punitive aspect. It might be disasterous, her disappearing now. She hadn't the smallest inkling that dinner was to have been Hugo's way of breaking off their friendship.

But cruel impulses must be mastered. He rationalized his cowardice with the thought that Octavia's holiday mustn't be spoiled. Nothing need be final.

Before he phoned again, Octavia had read in his cancellation a moment of truth. It all pointed to the fact that she'd attached too much significance to this man. He was too old. He'd always be ailing, letting her down. The vision of Russia had paled. Her fine adventure had become a shabby reversal in romantic fortune.

Then came his second call.

'I'm coming to see you. Don't expect the dashing figure of our last encounter.'

Arrived at the Cottage, he heard Roweena had retired to bed. 'She won't come down,' Octavia told him when he asked, almost indignantly, where she was. 'She's been depressed today.'

'Depressed? What about – your absconding?'

Octavia forced a laugh. 'Unlikely. She's quite hard to understand.'

Hugo said, 'I realize there's a sombre side to your mother. Is she ill?'

'No, she's not in the least ill.'

It occurred to him that this was a show of indifference hiding resentment, which in turn probably hid anxiety. 'Is she afraid of something?' They were moving slowly across the garden, Hugo inhibited by the sense that discussing Roweena with Octavia was less than fair.

'She's afraid of death. She dreads it.'

'Who doesn't? But don't you think she makes herself depressed talking about spirits the way she does? Rather a morbid preoccupation for a healthy person.'

'She's always had moods. They run in our family. Then there's that batty neighbour. Muth is pretty much in awe of her.'

'Is there something we can do?' Hugo wondered, though for the life of him he couldn't have said what. Certainly the Lily Falange woman seemed to wield an unsavoury influence.

He made his visit short, even felt himself eager to be gone. The bizarre atmosphere which had so intrigued him had palled. He couldn't contemplate that strange unhappy character upstairs and be calm. When Octavia goes, he promised himself, all this will finish.

'She's armed herself with loads of tins and is psyching herself up to having you for dinner when I'm home. Will you come?'

He said gallantly, 'Yes indeed – bringing a tin-opener if necessary. Meanwhile, I'll expect a postcard from Russia. I'm going to be busy myself. I'm glad. Life might have fallen a bit flat without you.' Steady, he thought. Steady.

This tribute brought a smile to her lips. He waved his hand as he went to the Rapier, blowing at the same time his suffering nose. He stooped to get in.

'Oh!' she cried, partly to detain him. 'I told you the wrong ship. It isn't Norma. It's Estonia.'

'Then what of the bouquets I've had sent to the Norma?'

Suddenly Roweena was calling brusquely from her bedroom window. 'What a terrible tease the man is!'

Hugo climbed hastily into the Rapier while Octavia, unsure whether to believe in the bouquets or not, watched him go. Her heart clenched tight at the start of his engine.

He hardly dared raise his eyes to the upper window. When he did so, moving forward, Roweena had gone and the window was shut.

Chapter 16

Roweena stood outside the travel agency as the coach rolled away for Tilbury Docks. A journey to the Iron Curtain and beyond had begun. Would she ever see her daughter again? Who could tell what malign influences might engulf her in that land of suspicion and intrigue.

After her initial anxieties, Octavia was in blithe spirits. They were a group of about thirty young people, mostly male and involved with education. The ship was modest and without class distinction. Octavia shared a cabin with two teachers of domestic science, and with Louise, who taught PE. She and Louise struck an accord. They noticed that Russian classics were already in circulation among the aspiring travellers, and chose themselves some Turgenev short stories from the library. They sat on deck reading, while an Irishman launched into a cycle of jolly songs, rapidly competed against by the Russian contingent who mourned to the strains of an accordion.

A fine misty rain fell. They were rendering Clementine – the Irishman galvanizing the rest. How young they all seemed. Octavia felt a spasm of longing for Hugo, watching the sea heave around their ship, glistening black with marble veining.

They docked at Copenhagen, and there was a short documentary film during which Maurice, a mathematics teacher, accused Octavia of being bored at mealtimes. 'Are you pining for a lover?' he enquired. She responded to his teasing and they became friends.

The ship paused at Gdynia and its passengers drifted round that desolate spot with gloomy curiosity. In the evening it drizzled and blew cold, an ominous swell roused up and gradually sea-sickness struck the hilarious voyagers. Octavia lay in a life-boat while a gregarious Israeli stole one of Louise's slippers and threatened to toss it overboard. His little pleasantry came to an end only when a green tinge swept his laughing face and he bolted for the rails.

The charms of the Swedish archipelago. Rocky timbered mounds, dazzling sun and visions of a splendid solitude.

There was a fancy-dress party their last evening aboard. Louise told Octavia that if she was prepared to be a Greek goddess she would put her hair up for her. Then Maurice passed on a tip from the Purser that someone should go as Peace. So wearing a halo and holding a sprig of artificial mistletoe, the Greek goddess won a bottle of champagne. During all the festivities their Captain sat dark and inscrutable in a corner, while the Purser sang a comic song about mealtimes, and they all roared the Volga boat song together. A popular member of the crew danced for them and his cronies joyously choroused, 'Good old Spartak!'

They approached Leningrad down a long canal encompassed by its great grey bay. Armament strips lay to right and left. Timber floated freely in the water. Enthusiastic greetings awaited them at the quay.

Driving to the Europa Hotel through streets that were clean and wide, but everywhere drab, Octavia saw it as not unlike the dingier outskirts of Paris.

They hung about in the Europa reception hall, staring at photographs of ballet dancers mysteriously grouped, or draped like puppets. A wall length mirror of monstrous proportions reflected their weariness. There was a lot of ornate plaster work and classical busts.

Finally they were allowed to disperse to their rooms, and Octavia thought of Hugo. She wondered what he was doing. Was he in London, or in Sussex? She hoped he'd call at the Cottage while she was away. Perhaps he and Nicky would go to the pub together. Now that Hugo had lifted her above reality as she'd known it, he seemed to be hers as of right.

They were driven over Leningrad in hot weather, disgorging at Saints Peter and Paul's Cathedral, the Hermitage and the Winter Palace. Always those weighty brownish buildings, wide squares, drab traffic, lack of polish, crude approaches. Seldom any children running along the windy streets.

She scratched on a card to Hugo, 'Leningrad has everything on the grand scale except baths. Just as you said! We all had showers today at Peter's Summer Palace which boasted 130 fountains. Romeo and Juliet last night (the ballet), concert tonight, Moscow tomorrow. I'm getting very friendly with Maurice who is humourless but nice. Our guide makes comparisons with the West, talks of the new freedom here, but has never been abroad.'

Hugo had asked for a card; it didn't occur to her to send him anything longer.

She went for a walk with Maurice and Louise. They rested on the base of St Isaac statue, receiving tentative smiles from passers by, while across the river gleamed the cathedral spire. Russians stared at the girls' short English skirts, and Maurice kept taking Octavia's arm.

They dined in the hotel restaurant where privileged couples sat eating almost stylishly. Maurice ordered beer and coffee. Hungry and tired, yet refusing to eat, he appeared loath to leave once the others had finished. A well-groomed German asked Octavia to dance with him, and all the while she thought how different Maurice was from Hugo. Moody yet straight-forward, he was like a brother already; while there were layers and layers of Hugo, constant surprises.

Their flight to Moscow lasted an hour, with enough sunshine to illuminate stretches of brilliant cloud above and below. It was a fast bumpy ride from the Moscow airport into the city, with vistas of squares, ponderous blocks and the lit tower of the university. Traffic seemed more conspicuous. There was even a modest display of strip-lighting. By the time they had all found rooms in their primly modern hotel there was a bantering consensus that the iron curtain was indeed no more than a diplomatic blind.

No sooner was Octavia settled in the hotel than she and Louise were hurrying with intrepid impatience into the underground system to explore Moscow. They emerged at the centre in rain, and found the Bolshoi Theatre, Lenin Library, Pushkin Museum and the Kremlin. Despite the weather they felt pleased with their tour and with themselves; until the moment for returning on the underground and they realized with a shock they hadn't the slightest recollection of their hotel or address. They stood helpless and inclined to laugh on the platform, while kindly and curious Russians hung about them, failing to understand.

This is serious, Louise kept repeating. She had visions

of vanishing into Moscow's sub-culture for ever. Octavia was unconcerned. She already felt protected by diplomatic immunity. Up in the street, she asked for directions to an In Tourist office. Finally, comprehension dawned on a young man who took them to one not far away. They reached the hotel late in the evening and found their poised guide agitated and angry. No-one had the right to disappear! Octavia bridled, then realized that the woman was afraid of reprisals. The domestic science teachers were inclined to be piqued, and Louise made things worse by finding their attitude highly comical.

Octavia wrote home and, separately, to Isabel. To her mother and Nicholas she reported, 'Toured Moscow in a downpour and visited the Kremlin which was shut to visitors. We went into GUM (Woolworths to you.) Books and records extremely cheap. There's hire purchase here and the apartment blocks are scaled to the Neighbourhood Principle with all facilities. You ought to come Nicky. You'd really impress the local talent and there are some gorgeous girls, whatever Olly said.'

What she wrote to Isabel was, 'All is trivia compared with collecting a letter from Hugo at hotel reception. I grabbed it, my legs folding up. The truth is, I love him! I adore him. I did the only thing possible and sat on the stairs to read his news.'

He had written, 'Dear Octavia, It has rained steadily ever since you left. The Conservative party has been split wide open by Macmillan's appointment of Lord Hume as Foreign Secretary. But none of this will be of consequence to one who is heedlessly preparing for a troika ride in the Devil's Forest. Some day you'll be sorry. You will miss the Chalk Downs, the tennis, the pub, bitter lemons after trespassing. You can't trespass in Russia don't forget, because everything is State-owned. Please take care, Octavia. You should never have gone on this trip in the first place, abandoning your mother to the dreaded Mrs F.

'On Tuesday I went to London to talk with some contacts at the BBC. They were thinking I might broadcast a series on South-East Asian minorities. But I don't see it happening this year.

'Can you dance the mazurka yet? Or cook a beef Stroganoff? I thought as much. Well, enjoy yourself. But remember that holiday romances are always a lot of nonsense. Love Hugo.'

She wrote back, 'I'm alive and well and thriving on red air.

But the start was grim. There was a ginger-bearded Bohemian, a husky Scot with be-daggered sock, a woman over six feet tall. Then I lost my suitcase. I was made an example of by the officials of Tilbury because my name wasn't on their list. All before I left England! I won some champers on board which I opened clad only in a sheet and I wanted to keep the cork for you, but it flew out through a porthole.

'The Sussex Downs seem tame after getting lost in Moscow. There's an exhibition of Russian Achievements – decrepit sputniks and radios. Ideal for your BBC series? I'm off to the Gorky Amusement Park now. Do you want a fur hat? Love Octavia.'

The British group toured prescribed sections of the university after which two reporters from Moscow Radio were eager to speak to them. They returned past the Field of Mars and a mosque. Quiet Russians were bathing along a central lido and some smaller canals in the suburbs, their faces uniformly blank. 'There are one hundred and one islands,' said their guide. 'We Muscovites know how to relax.'

And to the Bolshoi Theatre. Maurice murmured to Octavia, 'Do you realize you're the best-dressed woman here?'

The theatre was gold and white, with scarlet curtains and an opulent chandelier. The ballet was 'Taras Bulba,' national costume: all baggy trousers, boots, sashes, ribbons, sabres and bearskins. There was a lover who leapt from a real horse into his lady's boudoir down a spacious chimney. Octavia thought, I must tell Hugo ... Plenty of country scenes, murders, executions, stake-burnings and passion. The next night it was 'Prince Igor,' another lavish production with a preening hero – as handsome, their guide observed, as any heart-throb from Hollywood.

They returned to Leningrad, where Octavia and Louise raked the Nevsky Prospect for art books and prints. Octavia had set her heart on buying fur hats for Nicholas and Hugo but had left it too late. They all sang a version of The Lily White Boys as they journeyed to the docks.

This time on board they sat where they liked for meals and started with their best dinner of the tour. The Scot said, 'This meat is excellent. Perhaps they have an Angus cook.' To which Maurice, who had some humour after all, replied that perhaps it WAS the cook.

They paused at Helsinki and again Octavia sought in vain for fur hats, buying bottles of Georgian wine and vodka instead. She watched shooting stars up on deck with the tall woman, who talked of her research on vivisection and the depravity of medical students with whom she shared room in London. This exchange made Octavia reflect on her own plans to try for a job at API and live in London with Nicholas. That would fill the gap before the Foreign Office contacted her; and she'd live in London with Nicholas, who had still not found anyone to take Oliver's place in their flat. Life would be fun on all fronts. She'd be near Hugo.

A persistent chorousing of Moscow Nights began to tell on them. Going to the cabin to read, Octavia was challenged by a stewardess who waved at her pointed shoes in grim disapproval and wouldn't teach her the mazurka. Time began to hang. There was an entertainment by a Russian youth who gave an Elvis Pressley imitation. And the ship kept rolling.

Roweena met her train at Brighton. Octavia was so fatigued she could hardly bring herself to speak as they drove towards Fulking over the Devil's Dyke, and into the villages under the Downs.

Her mother was full of questions which largely went unanswered, moving between Russia and Sussex so glibly that Octavia shut her eyes. Lurching through Poynings, Roweena said, 'There's a surprise for you at home.'

Octavia ran hot and cold with pleasurable dread. Untrimmed hedges lashed the windows as her mother flogged the car uphill. Dust rose behind them. Roweena gave a happy chuckle. 'I've bought myself a doggie'.

Chapter 17

Hugo hung about the foyer of the Tate.

He wandered over to the postcard displays and swung their stands round and round. When Octavia came – with her friend – there'd be no clasping within arms, no special references or jokes. Their pleasure would hide behind facades, he decided. He'd let the other girl see nothing. He'd be a fool to act otherwise.

He was fool enough to be picking up the broken friendship after he'd dropped it. But how exuberant she'd sounded on the telephone! Infectiously happy, rekindling his interest in the way she perceived him. This simple, arcadian contact with a girl made him feel he'd been middle-aged always.

Were they very intimate, these two young women? More intimate than Octavia and he? Naturally. They would reveal not only their inmost secrets to each other, but their bodies as well. How had Octavia described him to her friend? A bit of a fuddy-duddy? A dashing Lothario? Any observer would pair off the two girls, not him and Octavia. They might even see a father with two daughters. He'd told her he regretted the fur hat more than he could say, but now he was glad. She'd have expected him to be wearing it.

He wasn't much interested in Picasso's paintings. That had been her idea. The friend was a devotee of modern art.

Someone touched his arm. They were both smiling at him, fresh and glamorous. His nieces, perhaps . . . he could better think of them as nieces. One was greeting him possessively, the other checking him out. He kissed Octavia, just for the hell of it. Miss Gibbs looked pleased. Greeting her, he was certain from her smile that he was shaking the hand of Octavia's confidante.

Hugo pushed a miniscule package at Octavia. He felt suddenly bashful and muttered, 'I got this from the shop here while I was waiting. Just for fun.'

It was a wooden mouse brooch with a leather tail. Octavia thanked him, thinking the gift and the giver both sweet and absurd, and pinned the brooch on her jacket. Then Hugo put loose arms about them and moved towards the exhibition, his fingers touching Octavia's hair so casually it thrilled him. Her hair was straight down her back, very long now. The other had hers crushed into a scarlet beret. How impregnable Octavia seemed when grave, and when laughing, how perfect! Decidedly it was madness to have fallen for this plan.

They spent an hour pushing around the crowded rooms and failing to agree over the paintings. Isabel would only discuss those she liked. Octavia studied each one carefully, and was enthusiastic in her comments. What Hugo liked was their debt to primitive art. That was something he could grasp in theory. The trouble was, for him, that Picasso's work was primitive without subtlety of form or colour. The girls were dismissive when he tried to explain.

He noticed Octavia's reactions when he stood long and pensive before one of the savage nudes. She tossed her head in the way he remembered, and said it was pathetic.

He gave them lunch in the basement restaurant, and told them how busy he'd been over the past three weeks, writing up the research he'd done on his previous expedition abroad. He was wondering if he'd ever be ready for the next trip. They responded with descriptions of Octavia's new job at API, and more information on the people there than he cared to hear. Isabel in particular seemed to regard work as a kind of game. He said, 'I believe I've met Max Fortune. He's a smooth operator. But don't be misled. He can be quite seriously difficult when he tries.' He asked whether the work at API would stretch their minds – prepare Octavia for a foreign posting, possibly in a war-torn zone far from civilization. They exchanged glances and hooted with laughter. Hugo said, 'At least you aren't competitive career women; and Nicholas in his flat will do well out of the swap for Oliver. Don't you think so, Isabel? If his sister cooks and cleans for him.'

Isabel's response was a feminine snort, but Hugo's attention had returned to Octavia. 'How did you square your mother?'

'No problem. She's got her heart-throb.'

'Oh?' Hugo queried. 'Now – who can that be?'

They giggled. 'A puppy.'

Hugo lay back in his chair, smiling about him. He let them chatter on. They were disagreeing over pictures again. He was entirely happy. What if he became Octavia's parent, her legal guardian? Now, there was a thought . . .

'You know,' he said, 'I don't see what you two are so steamed up about. According to my friend James Wedge, Picasso was over-mined long ago. To hear you talk, you've just invented him. You remember James, Octavia? 'The Way of the World?"

Chapter 18

Nicholas said, 'I expect you know Hugo's been married already?'

'Naturally.' Octavia batted cool lids. Was it brotherly concern, or brotherly malice?

Nicholas paid her the compliment of a curious glance. 'What's happened to your affair with Oliver since he came back from Spain?'

'Oliver's a pain, I always said so. The affair is with Spain as far as he's concerned – not with me. Isabel's showing signs of falling for him, by the way, so be warned.'

Roweena came in, nursing her dachshund. He lay like a roly-poly pudding along her arm and regarded his siblings with unconcealed dislike, daring them to set one foot wrong to know who was master. Nicholas only recently had trodden on him in the dark hall, an accident which the dog had taken in bad part.

'What shall I call my little orphan? Shall it be Tristan? Or Percy? Or Felix? They were all on my short list of names for you, Octavia. In case you'd been a boy.'

Nicholas said, 'Felix is the least objectionable – in case he'd been a cat, that is.'

He shuffled some foolscap pages in the air, knowing the dachshund was watching. Never fond of small dogs, Nicholas abominated this one, who tended to regard him with a bark ever poised between his jaws. Nicholas was thinking, dear old Hugo. He fancies himself a gay dog with my sister.

Roweena flung down some books. 'I'm improving my mind,' she said. 'I won't be outdone by my children. I remember you reading this Octavia. But really, that wretch Shelley! He fills me with irritation. He and Byron were as bad as each other. They needed their heads banged together. What a dance they led their families.' She sat heavily on a chair and trapped the dachshund's tail under her, so he nipped her. 'Little demon!' she cried. 'You're too quick. But you don't bite ME.' She tapped his long nose. 'I'm also reading poems by Wordsworth. I want to learn some by heart.' She massaged her bite. 'And Blake. Now there's a deceptive poet. Take his 'When I was one and twenty I heard a wise man say, Give crowns and pounds and guineas, But not your heart away.' There Octavia, heed Blake's warning. He was very astute for such a naïve man.'

'It wasn't Blake,' said Octavia. 'It was someone else.'

'Oh. Well, it might have been Blake. He wrote 'Love's secret – Never seek to tell your love, Love that never can be told.' The rest has gone – but you see my brain isn't quite rotten. I've been making changes in pencil here and there, I see no harm in it. I don't suppose I improve them but they seem to run more evenly. Perhaps I'll call this little rascal Byron.'

Octavia went into the garden and lay down in some long orchard grass. Above her head hung an apple tree. Small pink apples that brought back childhood.

Yes, Hugo had been married. He said the divorce had been sad, but inevitable. No children. End of story.

She chose to indulge in nostalgia. Nicholas singing 'Sheep may safely graze' in the upstairs passage. Reading 'Just So Stories.' Shooting with airguns. Playing bicycle croquet. Climbing into lofts, sprawling on haystacks. 'A Room with a View.' 'Shepherd of the Hills.' 'You are my Heart's Delight.' 'So Blue.' Old fashioned songs on their old fashioned gramophone. Foxtrot melodies of the Twenties era, with their innocently decadent spell.

She and Nicholas used to be inseparable.

There was something of a Thirties man in Hugo. She could see him on board ship in cruise clothes, while Thirties love songs floated in the air.

You know he's been married before?

Married how long ago? Married for love? In love again?

Chapter 19

Hugo was lazy. He knew he needed to keep reasonably fit but found walking without an objective a bore. It had been a bone of contention in his marriage. Vivian appeared to think exercise was an end in itself. He had ended up feeling somehow unmanly. Octavia was a refreshing change. He telephoned Fulking to see if she would be at home that weekend. She was. He planned a march over the Downs, this time to Chanctonbury Ring.

'You're wearing your Bardot vest,' he remarked. It was a blue, spacious day. He was not undistinguished himself, in tennis gear, heavy socks and army boots. 'Shouldn't you have a sweater or something, in case it gets cold?' Steady on, he silently cautioned. You're talking like her mother. Or was he? Roweena probably never bothered with such concerns.

They mounted the hills, hoping to find dew ponds. Octavia could remember one which she vaguely associated with fairies. Hugo looked quizzically at her when she told him. 'I'll bet there are no fairies there now. Only people with alternative proclivities. It's sad. Nothing is sacred.'

'That's the first time I've heard of alternative proclivities.'

'The expression – or the condition?'

She burst out laughing. He was being so discreet with her. She blushed slightly and didn't answer, shaking her head and still smiling, as though protecting his innocence rather than her own.

At Chanctonbury, standing in the circle of gigantic trees, Hugo said, 'This is a prehistoric site. An ancient hill fort. The trees themselves are probably hundreds of years old.'

'There's a beautiful hush in here. It's quite chilly.' Octavia shivered, feeling those past ages all about her. 'I want to go back to the sun.'

They lay in long grass below the Ring. 'You are ninety-two per cent perfect,' he told her.

'Really? What's wrong with the eight per cent?'

'I knew you'd want to know.' He pretended to consider. 'You're a bit too cocky at tennis.'

'You mean, I let myself beat you?'

'I mean you're too cocky. I played with James the other day and wiped the court with him. To begin with. It would have been a chastening experience for you to witness.' He gave a mirthless chuckle. 'Then I went to pieces.'

She demanded, 'Why don't you go to pieces with me?'

He rolled her over and kissed her. A harsh, dominant kiss. She was paralysed with excitement. Then he spread half his body the length of hers. The rough ground bruised one side of her back beneath his weight. She shut her eyes, hearing the jackdaws cawing overhead. Then very slowly, very deliberately, Hugo slid away.

Chapter 20

Roweena had pulled the curtains across. She'd tell them nothing of her intentions yet. She was afraid to explain them.

Isabel was asking everyone in general, 'What happens now? Do we establish atmosphere?'

'That sort of remark certainly creates one,' Nicholas whispered. Then louder, to his mother, 'Do we have to go through with this, Muth? None of us is keen.'

Hugo, his face inscrutable, was pulling dining chairs up to the table. He said to Roweena, his voice lending dignity to the occasion, 'Just the glass then, and that's all?'

Roweena approached, heavy-footed, and the girls grew still, sitting with hands folded and knees together.

Roweena said, 'Just the glass. I'll put out the letters myself. Oh where is Lily? How like her to be late!' There was a tap on the open door and a huge person entered the room. 'Ah, Lily. I didn't think you'd let me down. Give a chair to Mrs Falange, Nicholas please. That's right . . .'

Hugo introduced himself, shaking Lily's hand. Her grip was very plump and moist. She seemed reluctant to look upwards. She smiled towards Isabel and sank on to her chair. Although her eyes were downcast, they were very active.

Roweena said, 'We're grateful to you for coming Lily, with all you have to do.' She was still clutching the cardboard alphabet in her hands. Now she began to lay the letters round the table edge. When Nicholas tried to help she waved him aside, but Lily Falange took some of them from her as of right, and carefully rearranged several others.

Isabel whispered to Octavia, 'I know someone who played Planchette and jolly well went off their trolley.'

Roweena clapped her hands. 'We will begin.'

Hugo took a seat. In this prematurely darkened room, with the girls aquiver and Nicholas irritable, Roweena was almost sinister with purpose. The gross person beside him was breathing heavily. Hugo felt far from sanguine.

Roweena sat on Lily's right, with Nicholas beside her. Head bent, fingering one of the letters, she simply said, 'I'm grateful to you all for sharing this experience with me – for the moral support.' There was an awkward pause. Mrs Falange had her eyes closed. Roweena enlarged: 'It has to do with my husband, you know. The questions I want to ask don't reflect much credit on me, but . . .'

Nicholas made a gesture of remonstration. 'Oh now Muth, look here.' He shot a meaning look at the visitors.

'Quiet.' Roweena held up a peremptory finger. 'You don't have to say anything. The fact of your sitting here with Octavia might be a help. Believe me, I've made up my mind.'

'But Muth . . .' Again Nicholas did his best and was again cut off.

Hugo said, 'Let's see what happens,' dreading that above all things.

Isabel had grasped Octavia's wrist.

Mrs Falange said diffidently, 'You all know what you have to do?' Her voice was like a small girl's. 'Touch the glass lightly. No-one needs speak. If we contact anybody, I shall ask Mrs Ransome's questions for her.' She took a piece of paper from Roweena and scanned the lines of writing on it. They put their fingers to the glass.

Nicholas tried once more. 'I really don't think you need ask anything, Mother.'

Roweena glared at him, majestic in her stubbornness. Hugo regarded her with fascinated awe while Nicholas, crushed, replaced his finger on the glass.

Silence for a minute, except for the hump-backed clock ticking. Then to Hugo's surprise, the glass began to move. Hither and thither it shuttled, gaining impetus. When it seemed frantic for control, Mrs Falange's voice accosted it: 'Is anyone there?'

Her voice was suddenly deep and brusque. The glass checked, veered in a tight circle, then began to tack from letter to letter in lurches. Isabel stifled a nervous desire to laugh. Hugo held his breath. He was afraid his finger would slip. There was great suspense in the semi-darkness.

T O B L A T the glass spelt out, then subsided.

'Who is Toblat? Are you a man or a woman?'

The glass remained inert. Nicholas withdrew his hand. 'It's over,' he stated.

'Nonsense,' his mother contradicted with unexpected vehemence. Only Hugo's hand remained with her own.

Nicholas said, 'Toblat. That's Talbot backwards.'

Hugo gave a dry cough. 'I hoped no-one else had noticed.'

Roweena pitched forward at him. 'But how useful! Have you a particular relative up there, Hugo?'

'Nobody who couldn't spell their name.'

Relaxing, Roweena said, 'Please put back your hands.'

Again the glass grew animated, careening round like a thoroughbred colt. Lily said, 'May I ask a question about Roweena Ransome's late husband, Gilbert?'

The glass spelt Y E S

'Can you tell me, Toblat, was he ever – um – untrue, when he was alive?'

When he was alive. The phrase opened fresh queries. The glass spelt Y E S. Isabel's finger slipped off and she replaced it with a yelp.

Lily said, 'Can you tell me, was he untrue to his wife once – or many times?'

The glass didn't spell NO, as Hugo expected, but unequivocally M A N Y T I M E S.

'Did he have one special . . . can you tell me?' Roweena asked, hoarsely.

The glass spelt, O N E.

Roweena slumped a little in her chair. Octavia caught Nicholas's eye and thought he was going to object again. Nobody spoke. To break it off now, they all felt, would be worse than to continue.

'What was her name?'

The glass halted as if shocked. Hugo heard Roweena's breathing grow more intense, then realised part of the sound was his own. The glass, recollecting itself, shuddered and again set off doggedly, lunging into first one letter, then another, and spelling out V I R G I N I A.

'Virginia?' Roweena seemed astonished, as though any name but that had been awaited. But she was electrified with excitement. 'Virginia who, can you tell me?'

Again the glass appeared to consider, then circling wildly, it came to rest. They all kept their fingers steady with a concerted effort. 'Virginia who?' Mrs Falange repeated.

C R E E P E R the glass spelt. As one being, they removed their hands.

'Creeper?' Nicholas said. 'Virginia Creeper?'

'There must be some confusion with your garden,' Hugo offered, while Isabel began to roll about on her seat, Octavia and even Nicholas joining the mirth by degrees.

Roweena snapped, 'Be quiet, will you?' Her eyes and shoulders narrowed. 'How can you mock this thing? Do you want harm to come of it?'

'Definitely not,' muttered Isabel, her hysteria swiftly put down.

Hugo laid a hand on Roweena's arm and felt it shaking with an inner violence while Octavia, in a voice that attracted attention observed, 'What a complete farce! But I'm glad the spirits have a sense of humour.'

She became aware that Lily was staring at her, aggrieved to the point of hostility. Pushing back her chair, Roweena swept a number of the letters on to the floor.

'No. I don't think we should take it too seriously,' Hugo began, feeling cool and callous as a surgeon.

She shook off his consoling touch and with an unsteady laugh exclaimed, 'Didn't I get what I asked for? But I think I'd better gather my wits and bear them to safety.' She blundered to the door, changed direction and collapsed on the chintz couch.

'A drop of Arnica will put you right,' Lily said, heaving to her feet and padding to the door. 'I know where everything is.'

I bet you do, Nicholas thought. 'Pull back the curtains, Tave. Give us some light, for God's sake.' He stooped to help Isabel pick up the cardboard scraps. 'What a dotty idea, Muth. What prompted you to do it? Or shall I say, Who prompted you?'

Roweena raised an awkward hand.

Octavia at the window said, 'Why punish yourself, after all these years?' Seeing her mother's stricken posture, she added, 'As if it mattered what Dad got up to? He stuck by you right to the end.'

75

'What about some tea?' Hugo suggested, wishing the mundane initiative didn't have to come from him. One of James's Jakata pictures flashed into his head: Sakka Breaks the Sacrificial Umbrella and Ends the Evil Ceremony.

Nicholas said, 'Excellent idea, Hugo. Come on you girls. I can see from Isabel's face how she enjoyed it all.'

Isabel went to stand at the stripped window. It was darkening outside on this late summer evening. She switched on the lamp at her elbow. An amusing remark about Virginia Creeper came into her head but, aware of the risk, she merely said, 'That occasion will live in my memory, Mrs Ransome.' Then she went to join Octavia in the kitchen.

Roweena's head sank lower. 'There were other questions to ask. Perhaps we'll try again after tea.'

'Not on any condition will I let you play again,' Nicholas declared.

They listened to the friendly sounds of tea being prepared. Lily reappeared to place a tiny bottle inside the door, and then vanished again immediately. It seemed to Nicholas she was sneaking off with an attitude of You'll Be Sorry.

Hugo, also contemplating escape, was ashamed to see tears starting down Roweena's cheeks, and to hear her say softly, 'Where is my dog? Could somebody please find Percy?'

Chapter 21

With a feeling of masculine well-being, Hugo entered the API building.

He announced himself to Elizabeth the receptionist, who sent Eddie off with the message. Already Hugo was a familiar presence in that sedate establishment.

Eddie peered round Octavia's door with the news of Mr Talbot's arrival. Left in the hall with Hugo, Liz told herself that he and Octavia were at least as striking as any of the film stars framed on the foyer walls. This was the area where Liz reigned, and Eddie the office boy served her, they in turn adding to the secretaries' spurious glamour by running errands for them. Both Liz and Eddie had agreed that Hugo was 'lovely,' and took great interest in the fortunes of the supposed lovers.

Octavia came to find Hugo idling through the API promotional material displayed in the foyer. He had a bar of bitter chocolate in his hand and a small smile of irony on his lips. 'Come on. Today you're going to show me where you profess to work.'

She took him to the modest room she and Isabel shared, both working for Miss Carpenter. Across the passage, Max Fortune's personal assistant Norah had a large room. The policy of Miss Carpenter's secretaries standing by as contingency help for Max Fortune was seldom effected, for the simple reason that Norah kept his work to herself.

'Far be it from me to delay you and add to the pressure in here,' Hugo said, turning to Octavia, 'but it seemed terribly urgent all of a sudden to remind you that I'm collecting you at six this evening. Meanwhile, what about a quick lunch? Perhaps you'd care to join us, Miss Gibbs?'

Isabel grimaced, pointing to the door. 'I'm seriously tempted. But you see these film inventories.' She slapped a pile of papers. 'All to be typed for Madam in there.' She pointed to Norah's door.

'Octavia probably won't have told you, because Madam hasn't got it in for Octavia. She has for me though. It's like getting a second boss and not knowing which you're supposed to work for.'

'Work for neither. Come and have lunch.'

The door opened to admit Norah. She was a plump fair woman, not obviously dragon-like, but irritable in voice and expression. 'How long till you get those finished, Isabel? I really want them this morning. Excuse me won't you?' She nodded curtly at Hugo. 'Forgive me for being a spoilsport, but you know the rules. No visitors beyond Reception.' The girls were silent. Hugo murmured an apology. 'Oh, and something else. Mr Fortune has stressed that he needs you both to be familiar with his filing system. He thinks you're not sufficiently briefed. We'll have to put some time aside for it.' Smiling her brittle smile, Norah withdrew.

'See what I mean?' said Isabel. 'But we're safe, Tavia. The last thing she wants is to share Max's precious filing system with us.'

Hugo took Octavia to a pub off Jermyn Street which he called the Arbuthnot Arms for reasons of his own, and ordered ham pies, vegetables and ale. They sat up on tall bar stools to eat. 'A quart of ale is a dish for king,' she quoted, the tankard cold between her hands. The bar was reddish brown like the wood of a violin.

'Yes, I am rather kingly,' Hugo replied; and when he also ordered two rounds of crab sandwiches she didn't demur. His authority made her proud. 'A penny for your thoughts.' He peered into her face.

'You never pay for them.'

He protested, 'I do! You're the cheat.'

'I was thinking,' she said, 'that in another ten days, you'll be gone.'

'Only for the dry season. Not much more than a couple of months. Could be less, assuming all goes well. They'll keep mail for me at the Embassy if it can't be forwarded. Promise you'll write at least once a week.'

'I promise if you do.'

'You bet I promise. Don't look so pensive. Be pleased.' He tapped her on the shoulder. 'With my academic career none too bright, it's a good thing to have another book in the offing. Hoping this one materialises. Come on.' He was glancing at his watch again. 'We'll walk through Piccadilly Arcade, where one is forbidden to shout or whistle. Norah will report you if you're late.'

Going to a party in Pimlico, Octavia was in exultant mood. Hugo gripped her round the waist and wrapped her against him.

'Who are these people?' Octavia enquired. He didn't seem interested in introducing her to any of them. They left the party early, leaping into a taxi out of the rain. He'd decided to take her to James's rooms in the Albany.

The taxi dropped them in Piccadilly. As they strolled into the Albany, Hugo caught sight of James himself, vanishing through the rear courtyard gate. He said loudly, 'Did you witness James's exit? Napoleon deserting the Grand Army. Furtive blighter. He assured me he was off to the country by lunch time. I wonder what he's up to?' They mounted the steps in silence.

'Will James mind us crashing in here while he's out?' Octavia asked as they penetrated the hushed interior, and wishing she didn't worry on other people's behalf. It was so half-baked. Isabel never bothered.

'James lets me come and go when it suits. Relax. He won't be back now. That strange parcel-like object he was holding is his overnight case.' He established her in the drawing room while he went to make coffee. It came to him with surprise that she hadn't been in the Albany before. Only in his daydream. He heard her sneeze, and sneeze again.

'I like James's Eastern miniatures,' she called.

Hugo bustled back. 'Are you getting a cold? That's what comes of dressing for glamour.' He ignored her show of indignation. 'Of course you've no hanky. Here – take mine. The pictures aren't miniatures, by the way. They're temple banners, from Thailand mostly.'

'Do the monks sell them?'

'They're collectors' items. An old and gentle civilization is being systematically despoiled.'

'Well, I think that's hateful. They're rather fascinating though.'

She began to examine the pictures. Hugo was content to drink his coffee and watch. It gave him pleasure to see her absorbed, and to hear her comments. After a while he went to stand beside her, admitting he had a few banners himself, but nothing like the

79

quality of these, and the only one he'd bothered to have framed had been a present to his mother. Textiles were his speciality. He would love to dress her in Kelantan silk, or in a gold embroidered Laotian sinh.

Octavia's eyes kept glancing from the pictures to Hugo's face. She thought how much it varied. At times it seemed intensely pallid, his eyes bleak within their pools of shadow; at others almost ruddy, so that his eyes glistened brightly. Enjoying his paternalism, she stirred internally.

Hugo meanwhile was recalling their conversation over lunch, and the way he'd boasted about his book. His book? It would do nothing for the fragile communities about which he minded so much. Only fellow academics would read it, people with no influence whatever, and even they weren't really interested. Not that he cared any longer what they thought. Besides, what hard-nosed publisher was going to accept such a specialized book? They'd need a commercial sweetener, the sort of thing the CIA would be happy to manage with their flair for spotlighting their involvement. What good would that do his reputation?

But the poison went deeper, and it went back a long time. What was the West up to in Indochina anyway? If the French had got it wrong, what conceivable prospect was there of the Americans getting it right? And yet, if American intervention was intolerable, what was the alternative – the Russians? The Russians were so brash they made the Americans look sensitive. The Vietnamese, the traditional enemy?

'A penny for your thoughts?' Octavia said.

'I was thinking how pleasant it is to go to the theatre. To eat in a restaurant. Be baffled by Picasso. Wonderful, after the privations of field work. But without field work, it could become stale. There you are. Now pay up.'

'You never do.' She went across the room and picked up the figure of a Kinnari maiden. It was a strangely seductive creature, bare-breasted and half human, half bird. It still bore the traces of gilding. Octavia stared at it for a moment, unaware that Hugo was studying her. Then she glanced at him sideways. 'Also purloined from a temple?' she asked.

He went over and took her in his arms, hoping her trustful femininity would inspire him afresh. 'Would you do something to please me, Octavia?'

She still held the Kinnari, her expression enigmatic. 'Pay up?'

He regarded her with eyebrows slightly raised and his small smile. 'Yes. Let me take off your blouse.' He kissed her on the tip of her nose and kept his face close while her heart stopped. Withdrawing, and in encouraging tones, he said, 'Will you?' He fondled her arms, taking the carving from her and replacing it on the shelf.

Octavia looked away.

'I really want to. Darling.'

He unbuttoned and removed her blouse clumsily, while she stood in painful uncertainty. His glance roamed over her shoulders and lingered on her bra. He fingered the straps. 'Let me remove this,' he said softly. 'Let me,' he urged, still smiling.

Prepared to relish the procedure but deeply uneasy, Octavia felt him unfasten the awkward clips.

Hugo sighed heavily. He cupped his hands over her breasts, and going behind, drew her against him firmly. He turned her round. Without speaking, he unfastened her skirt and watched it drop to the floor. Lovely legs,' he murmured, stroking her thighs with increasing pressure.

Octavia's arms were raised. She flinched as he began trenchantly to peel the tights down her legs. But when he reached her ankles, she obediently stepped out of them. One foot, then the other. He stooped over and kissed her feet, each in turn. Kneeling, he touched her briefs.

'Hugo! I don't want you to.'

He looked up passionately, obsequiously, pleading. 'Don't be cruel, my angel. Only once. You're so beautiful.'

His hands over-powered hers. She hung on, almost hating him; but he brought the briefs down and scrambling to his feet, beheld her in wonder. 'You're like a goddess,' he said as though he meant it. She began to relax, flaunting herself, standing on James Wedge's carpet for his eyes to consume, allowing herself to smile. A sensual force was expanding within her, a magnetic desire for them to go further.

'Thank you darling.' He was collecting up the clothes. 'Perhaps you'd better put them on again. Truly Octavia, you are lovelier than I could have imagined.'

She wound her arms round his neck. 'I don't want to dress yet.'

'Oh yes, come on.' His tone was positively avuncular. 'Remember those sneezes. You shouldn't be getting cold like this.'

'But I feel so warm.' She kissed him on the mouth with heady fervor.

Again he restrained her. 'I love your body. But all that must wait. I mustn't take advantage of you.'

She spread her arms and, sinking back, drew him towards her. 'Not yet. Not here. There's plenty of time later.' Good God! Would she have him make love to her on the spot? Or in the Laotian prince's bed, perhaps? Without any warning, he hurried from the room.

Was he so highly principled, Octavia wondered? Or had he lost his nerve? HE wasn't standing in the nude. If only he had been. She quickly dressed, full of strong, conflicting emotions. He'd let her down, made her feel ashamed. Yet he had respected and valued her virginity. He had protected her from herself, from making a fool of herself, very possibly. By the time she'd finished dressing, her poise was restored.

He was going away. That was the worst thought. Another two weeks at most. For goodness knew how long. The waiting was awful. He'd seen her naked. She had offered herself to him. And in no time he would disappear.

Chapter 22

With less than a week to go before his departure, and when he should have been getting everything packed, Hugo decided to call at Buckland Crescent. He found Oliver making himself at home there, tall, bronzed, self-assured and speaking pidgin Spanish.

'Feel like a bit of genuine Spanish omelette? Cooked in the last twenty minutes? Still tepid.'

'Not in the least,' said Hugo. 'Thanks for the offer.' He wanted to add, 'Do I take it you've moved back in?' but feared the answer. Obnoxious young man.

Octavia came into the room. She was astonished to find Hugo, tidy in a sports jacket amidst the backpacks and articles of clothing Oliver had scattered since reappearing. Hugo looked uncharacteristically at a loss. Oliver, lolling across a chair, was fingering toast into his mouth. There was a stale-smelling saucer of cigarette ash on the floor, and the radio vibrated with Charlie Parker.

Octavia frowned at Oliver. 'How Nicky ever put up with you, I can't imagine.'

'Seen Isabel's place?' mumbled Oliver through a mouthful. 'Everything's relative you know.'

Hugo perched on the table with a forced smile. 'Thought I'd just drop in. Find out how you were. I was sorry to hear you'd been feeling unwell.'

Oliver licked his thumbs and knocked crumbs from his trousers. It was a bare floor, apart from two rumpled rugs. 'Anyone need a lift? I feel a touch conspicuous revving round the capital in a Land Rover. I've regretted flogging the dear old MG every damn day since I got back. Calamidad!'

'I'm mobile thanks,' Hugo said stiffly. 'Why was I under the impression that you'd removed to Spain for good?'

'Wishful thinking? Actually, I've every intention of returning.

A few extraneous factors have cropped up back here. But I'm pretty well focused now and all set to launch into the courier business. There's a comfy living to be made that way I do assure you – especially if you know a bit of Spanish and can knock off a guidebook now and then.'

Hugo inclined his head. 'Very good.'

Octavia was picking things up in a desultory way, not looking at Hugo. Had she really stood without a shred of clothing on, in front of him? That had been the last time they were together. It had actually happened. But to what effect? The memory didn't make her feel cheap; but his matter-of-factness did, and Octavia allowed her feelings to show. 'Have you driven up from Kemp Town?' she asked indifferently. He always claimed he hated London driving, never wanted the Rapier there.

It was her turn to be ignored. Hugo studied a poster fixed to the wall. It depicted an elderly man with a young lady on his arm, talking to a flower vendor. They appeared to be in an eighteenth century version of the West End.

'Like it?' Oliver asked. 'Isabel's influence. She confiscated Nick's Jerry Lee Lewis flier – which he inherited from me I may say – one of my most treasured possessions actually – and stuck that thing up.' He dug out his car keys and held them aloft. 'No takers, then? Must get off. I could kill for some fags. Well, so long you guys. Vamos entonces. Muy buenas tardes Senores!' He embraced Octavia and she put her arms round his neck. Then with a Latin flourish, he kissed her hand and went running down the stairs.

His eyes still on the poster, Hugo said, 'That elderly gentleman is certainly an inveterate lecher. The flower vendor is a willing accomplice to the crime, and the young innocent is not quite as innocent as she pretends.' He turned to Octavia.

'You mean she's been de-flowered already?' Octavia replied rather too quickly. She didn't like his manner.

'Miss Amelia is becoming cynical, despite that purity I've mentioned before.'

She took a second to follow the allusion, then looked displeased. Hugo continued, 'She's growing up. But she still lacks finesse. Is Australian sherry worse than Spanish? How long are diplomats stuck out in postings? Regrettable callowness really, in quite a smart girl.' He owed her a further commitment in emotional terms, he knew it. She was feeling uneasy. But he was blowed if he'd conform to a stereotype; to a courtship by numbers. He smiled at her.

She said, 'How superior you are today.'

'Is – Olly – here much?'

'Olly? He's only just over from Spain. We can't let him sleep on the streets.'

Hugo walked over to the door. 'I could.' He stood silent for a moment. 'Are you really unwell? Not a diplomatic illness?' He went towards her, offering his hands. 'Come on, Miss Sedley. I suspect what you need is fresh air. I fancied we might visit the zoo. How does that grab you?'

She grimaced. Reluctant to take his hands and be pulled to her feet, she said, 'You're miffed because Oliver was here. You let yourself down, being so patronising.'

'Well, he behaved as if he lived here. Silly young idiot. I take it you aren't ill at all?'

Octavia shot him a look. He stared at her angrily, then rattled the door knob. 'Why did I once suppose you were narrow-minded? You exemplify the sixties, and I'm the old stuffed shirt. I don't suppose your mother is narrow-minded either, come to think of it. Eccentric, yes. But if I told her that one of the Cunard Liners is notorious for homosexual stewards, I don't suppose she'd turn a hair.'

'I don't suppose she'd have a clue what you were talking about.'

'Are you coming, or am I as superfluous as I'm beginning to feel?'

'I thought driving around London unnerved you.'

'It does. I didn't come by car. I took the tube, then walked.'

She widened her eyes. 'Isabel will be amazed at your mendacity when I tell her.'

In spite of himself he felt affection returning. 'I rashly booked us for a show, as a matter of fact. A kind of farewell before our farewell tomorrow night, and our official farewell the night after that.'

'Which show?'

'You'll accuse me of being narrow-minded. Or at any rate, of limited intelligence. You know 'The Way of the World' eventually made it to the Haymarket? That disasterous Jenny Sendell. Well she's left the production at what seems to have been short notice. Whether on account of her crass acting, or a wish to deny audiences her presence, I don't know. The discriminating view is that her replacement is marvelous. Without La Sendell, the play will fold of course. But I'd love you to see it done properly, after our mixed experience in Brighton.' His cheerfulness grew as he warmed to his cause.

Alas for a happy memory at the Theatre Royal. Muth and James had been so content with Miss Sendell. Octavia debated, then gave him the smile of truce. 'I'd like to see it again.'

They went downstairs. He watched her check that she had her key before banging the front door shut. 'If we take the tube to Baker Street we could walk to the zoo through Queen Mary's Rose Garden. There'll be a second flush of roses if we're lucky.' He drew her arm through his. 'I learnt something interesting today, by the way. About St. James's Piccadilly. Blake was baptized there. Did you know that?'

'No, I didn't. Though I'm sure you'd find Muth did.' Her sarcasm was lost on him for an instant. 'She's an expert on Blake. I bet you didn't know that!'

Chapter 23

The rose garden was so beautiful they lingered longer than they'd intended. It became too late to see the zoo, and too early for the theatre. As the traffic built up, they walked hand-in-hand down Portland Place towards the West End. On the spur of the moment, they went into a bistro, footsore and hungry, split a carafe of red wine between them and didn't hurry the meal. Time and space had lost their limits since leaving Buckland Crescent earlier in the day.

While they were drinking black coffee, they noticed the clock. They'd missed 'The Way of the World.' Hugo suggested going back to the Albany. During the afternoon there had been an intensity between them which had to be resolved.

Octavia stared upwards as they entered the inner courtyard. The atmosphere was calm, grand, mute as usual. 'I hope James won't regret going away so often.'

'Not one of his indulgences – regretting. And yes, he is away.'

Hugo made them more coffee. As Octavia took hers she said, from one of the leather wing-backed chairs, 'Do you remember when we met on the train? I'm glad I noticed you.'

'I saw you first. Did you think it was very tedious of me to speak?'

'Oh yes: Did I want the window opened?' She stretched. 'Sublimely banal.'

'Rather urbane actually. Recall how I handed you your book. Damn – that picture's crooked.'

He got up to make the adjustment. It was the most alluring of James's temple banners showing the demigod Sakka, dark green, seated on a cushioned throne. His palace was indicated by a walled enclosure, planted with fruit trees and thronged with half naked attendants.

'The Tavatimsa heaven,' Hugo advised her. 'Apparently a

place of earthly delights.'

The seated figure could have been Hugo, chivalrous indeed, and the enclosure the inner courtyard of the Albany itself, its exterior only just hinting at the bizarre goings-on inside. Seeing the smile on her face, Hugo went to sit opposite her. 'Darling, there's something I ought to say. You know that I've been married already. It's over and done with now. But I need to explain a bit.'

'You don't have to.'

'Vivian and I never agreed on a way of life. We never shared friends successfully. And in fact, though I gave Vivian her freedom when she wanted to remarry, I was lucky to make the break so easily. There was another woman.'

'I see.' Octavia wanted to make the picture of Sakka crooked again, then stalk out of the room until his mood changed. She stood up.

Hugo pointed to her chair with a peremptory finger. 'Please sit down and listen. I used to visit Diana. She organized the woman's page of some magazine. Because Vivian took no interest in my work – no, that's not quite fair – because she took the wrong sort of interest, and generally let me down as I saw it – I persuaded myself I deserved Diana. She was a dear warm person, much less selfish than I. She knew it wouldn't last. But she was loyal. She gave me happiness during a not very nice period of my life.'

Hugo looked at Octavia. He was sure she wasn't attending. Perhaps she wasn't particularly interested. Don't lay it on too thick, he counseled himself. Don't put her right off.

She said, fractiously, 'Yes. So?'

'You mustn't bite your lip. I just want to be honest with you.' Hugo leaned on his knees, his back very broad. He gazed at her with eyes that were devastatingly sincere. Gradually he became aware that his ghoulish insistence was stirring a deep unease in her. The purple carpet with its Chinese rugs, the carefully clashing maroon curtains, the maroon couch and leather chairs, all so familiar, seemed suddenly alien to this conversation. He stared at James's two corner cupboards and the magnificent Chinese cabinet without seeing them, and heard himself say smugly, 'My conscience is clear that I never deliberately broke up my marriage.'

'Only spoiled your chances of another one.' She was working up a grudge. 'You look very complacent, sitting there.'

He protested feebly, 'I've never felt less complacent in my life!'

Octavia kept strategically upright and calm. Sensations were rising in her like tides under a full moon.

He said, 'You look so remote. So dreamy. I can't allow that, you know. I'm rather vague myself. But if you married me, I know we could make each other happy. We can give each other what we both need most.'

Her sensations now were like a surging wave with a deep undertow of laughter. She threw herself on him and kissed his cheek. Why the confession? In order to propose! 'Beloved Hugo, if we were married! But it's what I want above all else in the world. Surely you know that!' She subsided on to his knees. 'But what will Muth say? And Nicky? I wonder if this will make Nicky and Isabel decide to get married.'

There was a pause before Hugo replied. Then he said, 'Your mother is important. The last thing we want is to hurt her. After all, as you gather, my life has been far from blameless. We must make it right with your mother. That's our first concern.' He stared at some stains on the leather chair, as if searching for a clue. 'We'll wait a while, shall we? Just to be sure. I AM sure, you know. But let it be our secret. For a while.'

There she sat, flushed and happy on his knee. My God, he thought. If Roweena actually did have second sight, what would she be saying now? He could feel the dark crescents under his eyes.

Leaning back, he said chastely, 'Octavia, your love-making is like your tennis. It goes on and on and you never give up. What have you done with the kisses we put in the silver box last month?' It was imperative, with this girl, always to resort to flippancy before too late.

For the second time in this exotic room she was filled with awe at the way he could quietly put aside their physical impulses. She remembered Eddie proudly carrying six yellow rosebuds to her from Hugo at API. Hugo had been wearing a short black coat with velvet lapels that day. He'd cast about in her little office, ignoring the rules as he always did. Then Miss Carpenter had come in. He'd suavely raised his hat to her and disappeared.

He'd thanked Liz for her 'diplomacy' on one of his other visits, and gone. It was as though he never thought to see them again.

But tonight he had proposed! It had all been just the beginning.

'Kisses generally mature with keeping. Good quality ones,' she told him. Then slowly she went on, 'Perhaps you'd better speak to Muth when you visit Brighton. If there's time before you leave.'

'Yes of course. While I'm in Brighton, I will see your mother.' He squeezed her hand gently. 'But don't you dare let Isabel broadcast our engagement round the API. We'll do things properly, when I get back from the Far East. And we'll have that diamond set.'

Twisting on his lap, Octavia put her mouth to his, as if placing a seal on all that had been said. Her passion for him was threatening to overflow his restraint. There was no mistaking her intentions. She wanted to consummate the occasion, and it wouldn't be in this room, casually. Once more, Hugo thought of the four-poster.

He held her tightly and spoke close to her ear. 'I feel just the way you do. But we must control ourselves at this stage, mustn't we? Suppose it turns out that James hasn't gone away after all? He could come back at any moment. And you must get your beauty sleep. You haven't been well.'

He escorted her all the way to Buckland Crescent, as if he never wanted to lose sight of her again.

Bidding her goodnight, he said, 'You'll have to imagine how wonderful 'The Way of the World' can be. But think, darling. We can look forward to seeing it over and over together, in the future.'

He pressed one of the tickets into her hand. 'A keepsake of a momentous day.'

Chapter 24

They sat side by side in the summer house at the Cottage, their nostrils filled with the scent of geraniums. Percy lay at Roweena's feet, one eye open for threats to his person. It's strange, Hugo thought, the difference between these two worlds: the gaiety of London, where all should be dedicated hard work, and this cottage, this miniature paradise (as he'd once absurdly called it) where all was not as it seemed, and under the colours, the quiet stretched threads of tension. As Nicholas was fond of saying, it was a garden of maximum effort and minimum use.

'Really you see, I think Octavia's wonderful!'

Roweena conceded, 'She has her faults. But she is rather a dear thing.'

Hugo folded his arms and crossed his legs. 'She's unworldly of course. And very stubborn.'

Roweena held a small pot of geraniums against the sky, as though making a primitive gesture to the gods. 'Oh yes, Octavia's certainly that. And as I know you too well to lie, I'll admit she's a bit scatty. She gets that from me.'

Hugo smiled affectionately. 'In admiring your daughter Roweena, you must realize how greatly I admire you.'

Roweena didn't appear to hear him. The sense of his words reached her in the form of an echo. 'Oh, what a dear you are!' She put the pot down again, allowing it to fall over and startle the dachshund. The Egyptian bangles tinkled at her wrist. Sitting in the sunshine, her mind was heavy. She added, 'Octavia gets the stubbornness from her father. At least I'm a flexible being. Quite reasonable, I suppose.' She confronted Hugo, tapping his chest. 'Do you know what I like best in Octavia? Her nobility of soul!'

'It's interesting you should say that.' Hugo spoke lightly in an attempt to disguise a feeling that he'd been caught out. 'Yes, it occurred to me that she has some special qualities. I hope you won't think this interfering, but I should mention that if Octavia is accepted by the Foreign Office, she'll very possibly be approached by the Friends.' Roweena looked nonplussed. 'MI6 you know. As a matter of routine they'll weigh up her background, and it's likely they'd find it attractive. Father a naval officer and with an Intelligence background. Good family. Finishing school in Paris. Spies are such snobs, Roweena. I'm quite sure that the delay in her security vetting has a lot to do with MI6's interest.'

'I don't know what I think.' Roweena articulated one of her hearty snorts, then fell silent. 'I believe she'd enjoy doing something a little exciting. She can be very discreet, she's trustworthy. And she's neat. That says something about her character you know – innate neatness. But I couldn't bear her to take risks. I'm thinking of those warnings.'

'I'm thinking of Octavia's happiness. How she can best fulfill herself. I'm afraid she'd find the endless subterfuge depressing. I doubt if it would be exciting. Let me put it this way. Something tells me that sort of existence could prove damaging to her. It could spoil an innocence and directness in her nature. What is your view?'

She patted his hand. 'You're delightfully romantic, Hugo Talbot. Have a word with her yourself. I wish you would. She seldom listens to my views.'

He stood up because she did, brushing dog hairs and ash and fragments of earth off her skirt. They walked through arbours that leaned with wood rot. She was expounding on pesticides. Hugo felt he'd been diplomatic. The moment of reckoning was deferred. He'd expressed his concern for Octavia as a friend – or as a lover. He'd be going abroad with his options still open.

After a separation of three months, who could say how he or indeed Octavia might feel? He escorted Roweena like a courteous gardener, seeing her as a gadfly, evading the threat of insecticide sprays, for ever just out of reach.

'I've been planning to ask you for a night sometime when Nicholas is down and I could have given you men a proper meal. When you get back from Indochina perhaps? But it's the bathroom. So awkward with a man. I don't count Nicholas. Having a man in the house is such a snag. But then, you live very near. Not like coming from London.'

Heaven forbid – a weekend closeted here! Intimations of locked doors, flushing cisterns and feminine distress on the landing. But there were other loos ... It might have been fun. 'My abiding worry,' she was saying now, 'is that woman who came for the Planchette. You met her – Lily Falange.'

To his surprise, his arm was gripped and he found himself impelled back into the summerhouse. 'Sit there, and just tell me Mr Talbot,' she said, the formal address quite unconscious. 'Tell me what you would do if you were plagued by another person?'

He said humourously, 'But I'm for ever being plagued by other persons!'

Roweena's face looked sallow, her eyes saw beyond him into the garden. She squeezed his arm. 'D'you realize that the monstrous Falange woman has organised her spirits to invade my mind.'

'I don't understand.'

'I'm tormented! I don't sleep. Shakespeare knew. He knew. I'm wading through him when I have time and energy. He understood. My daughter takes me for an ignoramous, of course.' She grew tense again. 'She – Lily – tells me that Gilbert resents my seeking the truth about him. The truth to which I'm entitled!' Roweena broke off. A bee was humming near Hugo's shoe. Birds fluted just above their heads.

'I'm sure a game of Planchette never put anyone in danger,' he said. What morbid conversations on this mild, bright day, when they might have been talking weddings. 'Perhaps you're run down, Roweena. Could your doctor help?'

'No.' She shook her head vehemently. 'Don't you see? If Gilbert resented my still being alive, with the garden, and my love for little Percy – then what chance have I for happiness or health? Lily repeats her rigmaroles from the German doctor – nonsense about a passing-on in our family. But I've decided to dismiss it all. I'm perfectly well, perfectly strong. If you want the truth, I'm beginning to think she's resentful because we laughed. We did, you know – and she may have thought it was directed at her.'

If ever I marry Octavia, Hugo thought, it will be to save her from this madness. But as though infected himself, he felt drawn to the mother with a deeper fascination. He fought a powerful wish to hold that healthy, untidy body and breathe comfort into it.

Roweena thought, This man will help me. He's full of common

sense and compassion. She said, 'Gilbert and I created our garden from scratch you know. It was nothing but broken glass and a sea of nettles when we first came here. I think it's rather successful, don't you?'

'Very successful,' he assured her, concerned at the way her eyes were again staring beyond him. Her distress reminded him of how she'd been after Planchette, and he'd resorted to making tea. He suggested going indoors for tea now.

'It's no good talking, whether outside or in,' Roweena said fretfully. 'There's no escaping the spirit world. They will have their little jokes. I shall go to my room, I know you'll excuse me. I can't bear to sit and talk about nothing.'

'Better that, than brooding on your own.'

She began going towards the Cottage. She didn't wait or bother to see if he came, but hurried through the front door. Percy trotted in her wake, with a sly backward glance.

Hugo told himself, I could just walk into the lane and never return.

He followed her inside.

Two days later he flew out to Bangkok, on his way to to Xiengkhouang.

Chapter 25

'Percy's unwell.'

Roweena lowered herself into a chair with the despair of a Jenny Sendell. She placed her hands over her eyes.

'Well, don't cry Mother,' Nicholas said. 'It's unlikely he'll die. He's simply over-fed, short-legged and broken-winded.'

'I'm not crying. I'm considering.' She was thinking, might Percy be a victim?

Isabel came into the room, freshly changed out of tennis things. She glanced at Nicholas who now seemed engrossed in the Financial Times. Then at Roweena. 'Oh Mrs Ransome – have you a headache?' She crouched at her hostess's feet.

Roweena replied from behind her hands, 'No no. Just sending up a little prayer for my dog. He isn't well, you see.'

Isabel thought, It's the easiest matter in the world to upset Nicholas when he's in his blazer. I wish he wouldn't insist on wearing it.

'Percy vomited his bread and milk.' Roweena laid an absent hand on Isabel's sleekly groomed head. 'How hot you are, little Isabel.' She took her hand away. 'Are you ill too?'

'We've been playing tennis Mrs Ransome. Nicky isn't hot, he plays a dilettante game. He isn't in my league at all.'

'Get Lily F to intercede for Percy,' Nicholas proposed, to put Isabel in her place. The grisly ramifications of a one-sided love!

Roweena shrugged. 'A spirit doctor isn't a spirit vet. I wouldn't want to offend the good man.'

'Why not a mortal vet, Muth?'

'The man's a brute. I wouldn't have him touch Percy if he did it free of charge. I've dosed the little fellow with arnica, and I hope he'll go to sleep'.

Nicholas flicked his newspaper as though her words had alighted on it like flies.

"Let's all go to church,' Isabel suggested, who preferred things to happen. 'Like people in the olden days.' She glanced humourously at Octavia. 'Coming, Tavia?'

'I don't feel up to it.' She could hear Hugo saying, 'Always examine the outside of a church first. And remember: go round clockwise. It's bad luck to go round the wrong way.' She'd wander after him between the tombs, his words washing over her while she read the inscriptions.

Her mother remarked, 'Religion consists of one's thoughts words and deeds. I don't need to go to church to be told that. But I need regular supervision. I need to be conducted into a receptive state.'

'I wish church services didn't have to move with the times,' Isabel said to her. 'I much prefer the old-fashioned prayer book service, don't you?'

Roweena flapped languidly in her direction. 'Yes I do. In that respect we're still old diehards here, fortunately. Personally, I balk at any change from tradition. I love our Poynings church.' She went to a console table and jettisoned the flower arrangement into a plastic bag. 'Don't dead flowers smell filthy?' Rubbing slime off her fingers, she turned to Isabel. 'Change makes me fearful. It becomes synonymous in my mind with loss. Don't touch those things, Percy. They're nasty.'

'What primitive logic, Muth,' Nicholas said. 'Tantamount to blasphemy! Now, if any among us are really game for a sermon, we must get cracking.'

Isabel jumped up. 'Octavia can stay if church makes her squeamish.' Tavia was pining, of course. Poor old her. But it was a mistake. She'd be better in company, putting in a good word for her beloved. Isabel wondered why Nicholas was so keen to go. He could have suggested a walk if he'd wanted, and got her to himself.

Roweena was tapping the hump-backed clock. 'I remember my mother winding the clocks in their house, and setting the time by the clock on the tower of Hove Town Hall. She used to look at it through binoculars from a bedroom window. That dear, red brick Town Hall! I knew it from my earliest childhood. The bells would play 'Where and oh Where has my Highland Laddie Gone' at every hour. Or was it the quarters? And those big red buses used to grind up and down Church Street, I'd listen to them at night, such a comforting sound. And Mother would tell her story of little Freddie who got stuck on the gasometer.'

Isabel was eager to be off, as though some brilliant piece of entertainment were at risk. She brushed aside Mrs Ransome's reminiscences. 'Don't slack now, Tavia. You can do some housework while we're gone.'

They went casually into the hall. Roweena looked in again. 'Darling, could you please keep an eye on the joint, if you happen to think of it.'

From her bedroom window, Octavia could see wooded country all about her, purple touched with bronze. She could almost smell the drenched leaves that spurted liquid mist beneath the feet. She watched Nicholas help his mother into the Morris. She watched them rumble away.

Chapter 26

Hugo wrote, as he had promised, as soon as he reached Vientiane. He sounded a happy note.

In fact he was disturbed by what he found. Helicopters with US markings were constantly overhead. These belonged to the so-called White Star teams – officially advisors, in reality American special combat units. There was little evidence of White Star personnel on the streets of Vientiane. But there were CIA operatives everywhere. Previously there had been one or two agents, notorious for their flamboyance. By avoiding them Hugo had been able to reinforce his own credentials. Now it was impossible to avoid contact. The town bristled with agents with other affiliations as well, many of them extremely threatening. Knowing that his movements were being watched, and his correspondence almost certainly monitored, Hugo had to treat his letters to Octavia as part of his disguise.

The Constellation Hotel was where he was staying, and its name headed the large crackly paper he used for his first letter. Vientiane was as delightful as ever. It was in some ways like coming home, he wrote. There were changes of course, not all for the better, such as General Phoumi's reckless bull-dozing of the Boulevard Circulaire. But the people were the same, with their smiling open faces, the absence of urgency or artifice. The climate at this time of the year must be the best in the world: bright days, cool nights, the ground drying out after the monsoon. La Saison des Chasses. It's also the campaigning season, when military activity resumes. Once in the mountains he'd be away from all that. As if deliberately lightening the mood, Hugo went on to say he'd visited the Morning Market and bought himself a sarong in black and white and red checks which he hoped she'd approve, and a couple of custard apples – a fruit that was disgustingly sweet. 'I expect to be on my way to Luang Prabang in two days,' he concluded. 'Letters from there may take longer, as I shan't be able to use the Embassy system. Meanwhile, what shall I be up to? Well, I expect I'll spend this evening with a Reuters man I've known over the years and whom I found knocking around at the Constellation. There's another old friend, an Egyptian WHO doctor staying at the Settha Palace Hotel. Shared dinner and a lot of old memories with him last night. So I can't claim to be on my own, darling. Nevertheless, I miss you terribly, and it's all just so much distraction until I can get on with my project – and until we're together again.'

Octavia was unsettled by this letter. She sensed he was not being frank. But that wasn't all. She realized that there was still a part of her which wanted to be accepted by the Foreign Office. Yet – supposing she were? It would be on the understanding that she was prepared for a posting to a British Embassy or Consular post anywhere in the world; which had held such appeal for her. How could she give that guarantee now? The last thing she wanted was a long engagement. And, as Hugo had suspected, a number of covert enquiries into her background had been made. She'd begun to dread hearing from them. As to where she and Hugo would live, or make their base, such questions still seemed premature.

Life was becoming difficult for Isabel too, and more immediately. She'd been moved to the inner office working for Max Fortune under Norah's supervision.

This morning, Norah bustled to the desk, dumping her handbag, divesting herself of her suit jacket. 'Had a good weekend Isabel?' She strained sideways to examine the heel of one stocking. 'Seventeen and six down the drain!' She jabbed a thumb at the communicating door. 'Is he in yet, Sweetie?'

'I don't know Norah. He hasn't buzzed.'

Norah said coolly, 'Well, he wouldn't buzz for you anyway. Let's hope he keeps quiet today. I don't mind telling you dear, I feel rotten. One of my sciatica attacks on Saturday, and yesterday I had my sister's two boys. They're nice lads but they always want sporting Aunt Norah to entertain them ad nauseam. Didn't do my back much good.'

Isabel murmured, 'Poor Norah' as she removed her typewriter cover.

Norah thumped about, examining the mail as though each envelope might contain a hate letter directed at herself. She said dryly, 'Don't make me feel too sorry for myself. And don't be upset if I'm a bit of a bitch today, Sweetie. This pain is a plague. Of course, he'll never sympathise over-much, in case I feel encouraged to stay home and recover. Do you know, in all my eight years working for him I've only been off sick once? Then he sent me an armful of flowers!' She sank down. 'Bloody Monday morning. I'm not neurotic, but the pills my doctor gives me don't help.' She threw a quizzical glance. 'Wake up Miss Gibbs. Dreaming of your young man?'

She lit a cigarette, an early morning privilege she reserved for herself. She didn't offer Isabel one. Slowly she filed the mail, a task she also reserved for herself. Seeing Isabel doing nothing she said, 'Wish I knew how many sheets of dictation we were in for. I got through ten sheets one day, on my own. Wish he was still in Luxemburg don't you, Sweetie?'

'I certainly do. I say Norah, you're very critical of Max. What do you really think of him?'

'Oh, you know me. My bark's worse than my bite. I'm quite fond of him, but I won't be a boss-idoliser. What's more, I'm the same way he is. I'm loyal to my own interests.' She switched a brittle smile on Isabel. 'Just pop through to the pantry and see if he remembered to bring us our coffeepot.'

Isabel obliged. This was her third day of initiation. She'd been quick to realize that Norah preferred to be alone in the room when Fortune looked in, so she could be the first to be called. Isabel returned with news that the coffeepot from Luxemburg was duly waiting for their mid-morning break. Norah drew on her cigarette in a masculine manner. She cocked an ear at Fortune's door.

He came through with athletic vitality and immediately threw open a window and shouted to his driver in the yard below. He spoke to Norah. 'How are you today Norah?' Standing still, he had a limp posture but his eyes were active. He wore an expensive cardigan.

Whether his query was intended as a courtesy or whether he felt genuinely concerned wasn't clear, but Norah took it up. 'To be frank, bloody awful.' She scowled playfully at him. 'I'm only kept alive with prescription drugs, you realize.'

Max Fortune said simply, 'Borrow my heat ray lamp.' He used this lamp to touch up the tan he acquired on his trips abroad. He took pains to maintain his figure, as the father of three teenage children. Isabel was learning a lot about his personal habits from the recorded 'sheets' she transformed into letters to his extended family.

'Did you find my coffeepot?' he enquired.

Isabel thanked him at once. Norah just grunted. She'd suffered bad coffee for eight years. Fortune regarded Norah with ironic disgust. It was as if she were his wife, thought Isabel, and he wanted her to know he was ashamed of her. Yet she felt he admired Norah, readily tolerated her, and was generous at heart.

He asked Norah to discuss his morning's activities. On her way into his office, Norah nudged Isabel with fierce condolence. 'That means you'll be getting the extra dictation!'

All too soon that moment came. Fortune waved Isabel to a chair with mustard velvet upholstery. The furniture in his spacious study was reproduction Louis XV, with a great deal of gilt. He had a marble topped table with ormolu fittings and long-stemmed bowls on it. There were life sized statues in a dim recess. The lighting was more Hollywood drawing room than office. Along one wall was a divan smothered in animal skins. Fortune sometimes spent nights here when the pressure of work was high. One of the first things Norah had told Isabel was that he was devoted to self-interest, but Isabel wasn't so sure. He seemed so involved with his wife and family.

Fortune dashed off a few notes. Isabel coped as best she could, trying to keep up her cool manner. He began to pace the carpet, his feet silent on its soft pile. He made a telephone call to his sister. Isabel waited, feeling like a governess in a wealthy family, and received some insights into Mrs Royston's private affairs. At last he returned to dictation and she covered her notebook with more hectic scribbles. Then she was politely dismissed.

Back at her own desk and with no wish for Norah to gloat, Isabel sat and puzzled at her shorthand while it was still fresh in her mind. Norah kept interrupting with remarks about Nicholas and Oliver. Then it was Octavia's private life. She was for ever passing comment on Hugo. If it was good old Auntie Norah longing to advise, Isabel wished she'd be less nosey.

Norah continued to suffer pains in her back for two days. She bit Isabel's head off, but was always able to shed light on Fortune's most obscure muddles. She had an intimate knowledge of all his relatives. If Isabel stuck over a niece's name, or the district in Yugoslavia where Mrs Royston's younger son was on holiday, then Norah would supply it. No tangle made by Isabel was beyond her.

One afternoon the following week, while Isabel was with Fortune, Norah came in. Her face was putty-coloured and moist. She treated Fortune with such brusqueness that he was forced to notice.

'Is something the matter, Norah?' He caressed her with his smile.

'Oh, nothing's the matter. Everything in the office is lovely!' She banged some papers in front of him and he sat back like a docile child receiving porridge. 'Forgive me if I'm not all sweetness and light, but my sciatica's put me in hell.'

'Heavens above, this won't do!' Looking from one to the other of his females, Max Fortune placed his hands on the desk. 'What would you like? For me to give you the afternoon off?'

'Of course my doctor tells me to stay flat on my back all day. And doctors are supposed to be realists. But a few hours might be better than nothing.'

Isabel nearly leapt up to clutch her and cry, Don't go!

Fortune rose and saw Norah to the door. Isabel suspected he was quite nervous of her. 'Get your coat and go home. Shall Joe take you in the Volvo?'

Norah accepted gratefully. Fortune came back. He and Isabel were on their own.

Chapter 27

Isabel survived the afternoon. But she was eager to greet Norah the following morning. There were problems she wanted her to sort out, and a file she had assured Fortune couldn't be traced. She came to an empty room. But Norah was occasionally late. Isabel hung around for ten minutes. Then she noticed some work waiting for the Dictaphone. On top of this lay a handwritten note: 'Norah is indisposed. Please carry on as usual. If you have difficulties, don't hesitate to ask.'

Isabel was transfixed. She was tempted to nip into Octavia's room. She longed for a cigarette. She wished Nicholas would appear the way Hugo did, and carry her off. Noises next door brought her to her senses and, visualizing a pile-up of work at the end of the day and no-one to share it, she moved into action.

The Dictaphone became temperamental. It wouldn't play the tapes loud enough – or possibly Fortune had been whispering, for a joke. She played certain phrases over and over again. A hot flush suffused her face. She couldn't hear! How could she be expected to take down letters that sounded like rats chewing? She sought relief in anger. She glowered at Fortune's door. It opened.

'Hello Isabel. I'm in a terrible rush. Please fetch the file I wanted yesterday.'

Not inclined to seek help as he had urged, Isabel was thrown into steeper decline. He'd already gone, and she hadn't opened her mouth. The machine crunched miserably to itself. She began circling the room, talking aloud. She couldn't find the file. Why was Norah's system so baffling? If Fortune was party to it, why couldn't he find things for himself?

He reappeared, looking annoyed. 'I told you I'm in a hurry. Mr Beverley's waiting for me in his office. Have you the file I asked for?'

'I'm afraid I still can't find it.' How sulky she sounded, despite the veneer of calm!

'But why not? Norah always sees the files are put back. Surely she's explained everything to you?'

His voice grated on Isabel's nerves. Ghastly affected man, couldn't he realize how awful he was being? 'No,' she lied. 'Norah's explained nothing.'

Well, it was Norah's own fault. It was treacherous of her to stay away.

Fortune's eyes narrowed in disbelief. 'I told her it was priority to teach you the filing arrangement. What do I do if only one person understands it?' He pushed past her and strummed along a row of files. Isabel watched with malice, hoping he wouldn't find it. But he did, and hissing, 'You'd better get Miss Carpenter's girl to help you,' he rushed away.

Octavia, composedly writing to Hugo, came to Isabel's aid as if she had been invited to share a joke. Together they stood at the Dictaphone, and together they declared themselves beaten. Then Octavia had an idea. She'd fetch Eddie. Besides being human, he had a way with machines.

He came to the rescue exuding confidence, delighted to have an opportunity to spend some time in a room he rarely visited. He put the machine right almost immediately. Then he embarked on an explanation of how it worked. Isabel's feelings of gratitude turned sour. Pointed thanks saw him off, and the two girls went back to work.

It was a feverish morning, and they forgot their lunch break. Octavia left Isabel to decipher the Dictaphone. She concentrated on getting the register up to date, and on mastering Norah's system of folders. She also took over the telephone, a rash move as callers all wanted information Isabel didn't have and Octavia couldn't find. More than one consultation with Norah proved necessary in avoiding disaster. Isabel showed no scruples here, but Octavia hated Norah's patronizing tone. One thing which Octavia quickly learnt was that Norah's filing system was less intimidating than it appeared. The folders were a strength, their picturesque titles proving an excellent guide to what they were likely to contain. If she could only persuade Isabel to consult them properly and to keep them tidy. Isabel's method was to put everything into a bulging General folder, which Octavia came to treat as the folder of first resort.

As though to add to their enjoyment, Oliver telephoned, threatening to call in and check out the scene. Isabel confessed that he'd taken to ringing at odd moments and she regularly called him back. She suspected he was aping Hugo, and thought Octavia would find this amusing.

'I sometimes wonder if he'll ever grow up,' she went on complacently. 'There was a time when he was responding rather well to you, I thought. You brought out the man in him, and you certainly looked glamorous together.'

To Octavia the idea of Oliver in the API was intolerable. 'He suffers from comparisons with that other person,' she told Isabel curtly. 'Come on, you get out and have some lunch quick, while I cover. There's still time. Then I'll go before the momentum builds again. And for heaven's sake, put the folders away in future. I veto phoning Norah ever again. It makes us look so feeble.'

Chapter 28

Norah was away for nearly two weeks. During her absence, Isabel valiantly struggled on with Octavia as her second-in-command. Very often Miss Carpenter's demands on Octavia's time left Isabel alone on the field of battle. This lunch time it was Octavia's turn to go out first after another hectic morning. Isabel typed on steadily.

Fortune emerged from his room. 'Have you the letter for Mr Rochester?'

Isabel went through her pile of finished letters. It wasn't yet typed. She gazed at him. His face was hard as a mask. How could Norah have given this man her allegiance? How could his wife have married him? Older men! What did Tavia see in them?

'Well, type it at once and bring it to my room. Eddie will be waiting to deliver it by hand.'

The letter was two pages long and fraught with queries. Isabel had to brave his presence several times and he helped her grudgingly. The letter he finally received was of the most squalid standard. Then, reinserting the letter which Mr Rochester's had displaced, she managed to reverse the carbon so that her copy came out on the back. She was near to tears. Her typewriter was thick with crumbs of rubber. When Octavia returned she found Isabel too depressed to take even a short lunch break for herself. Bless Fortune, Octavia thought, for eclipsing Hugo, and stopping me from moping.

Norah reappeared in the office not a moment too soon. The rest of the week passed with varying degrees of strain. Isabel perfected a system of nipping into Octavia's room, where she'd be given a bracing pep talk. Sometimes they managed a conversation about Hugo. Octavia was weathering his absence pretty well, Isabel thought.

That morning she'd caught Octavia engrossed in what was

clearly a letter from abroad. 'Come on, read it out,' she demanded. 'You know I want to hear what he's up to.'

'It's actually not all that cheerful. Things don't seem to be going too brilliantly.'

'But he's all right, isn't he?' Isabel waited impatiently. 'I'd really like to hear. Come on, Tave, before I'm called away.'

Octavia scanned the pages. 'Well, I think he's all right. Just fed up with the way things go on. He's been holed up in Vientiane at least a fortnight, when he'd banked on getting up north. No clearance from the security police. In fact, nothing seems to have been as straight forward as he expected. Apparently there have been awful changes, mainly bureaucratic by the sound of it. His health's not in great shape either – though he dismisses that as incidental.'

'And he's still in Vientiane?'

'No, he unexpectedly got a lift to Luang Prabang in one of the American White Star helicopters. Military advice people, or something. Hugo finished the letter at the airport and sent it back with the crew to be posted. Expect that's why it arrived so quickly.'

Octavia read silently from the letter: 'It will always be difficult living away from you. I don't expect it ever to get easier.' That was all right. But why did he add that he'd never found partings from Vivian easy either? Octavia was left with an impression not of a grieving Hugo, but a Hugo lonely for Vivian; and possibly for the Diana woman. She began to wonder what sort of future Hugo envisaged in which she and he were constantly apart and missing each other.

'I'd better go,' said Isabel nervously. Opening the door, she pulled up short. 'Oliver! Why are you here? Go away!'

'Come to see the chamber of horrors. Kept the morning free specially.'

'Get out of here. Go back to Spain. Perjure yourself somewhere else.'

Oliver took Isabel by the arm. 'Show me,' he urged. 'Please!'

Octavia was left alone with her letter.

In Fortune's outer office Norah was nowhere to be seen. Oliver surveyed the room. 'Stinks of nicotine. Not a bad size though! No wonder you wanted me to see it.'

'I didn't want you to see it. But since you're here, pass me that file. Under Locations. The one with John Rochester on the cover. Then, out!'

Oliver roamed the walls, whistling. 'There's no such file. You're teasing. Hang on though . . .' he pulled down a thickly filled folder. Some of the documents fell out. 'Rochester, you said? This is it. There's a chit signed Rokeby, will that do?'

The door opened. 'Well!' exclaimed Norah 'Feel free. Introduce me, Miss Gibbs.'

He said, 'I'm Oliver. Just off. Glad to meet you.'

The other door opened and Fortune walked through. He stopped halfway to Norah's desk and cocked his head. 'Are you the technician for the copying machine?'

'Not at all.' Oliver looked startled. Fortune waited, eyebrow quirked. No-one spoke. 'I was looking for Mr Rochester in Locations,' said Oliver at last.

'Really?' there was another pause. 'Then go to Canning Town. Berkshire. Anywhere.' Fortune went to the outer door and nodded.

'Cheers then,' said Oliver, and slipped through.

In silence, Fortune returned to his room, Norah dropped into her chair and Isabel studied the John Rochester file without seeing it. You had to be young to have fun, she told herself. You had to be young to live in the present.

When Norah started lecturing her about the sanctity of Fortune's private office, Isabel's mind strayed into realms of fantasy, seeing Hugo come into Reception in his velvet collared coat, joking with Liz, dispatching Eddie with a carnation for Octavia. Had the thought really occurred to her that Oliver might behave like Hugo – and she receiving his carnations? Some hope! Oliver was nothing but a pest, she decided. He had none of Nick's reliability and decency. Max Fortune wouldn't have imagined Nicholas was there to mend the copying machine.

And why, Isabel asked herself, was Octavia so damn secretive about Hugo? What was in those letters she kept hiding away?

I must get hold of them next time I'm in Buckland Crescent, she thought. I simply must read them and see if I'm right. For the idea had come to her that possibly, just possibly, Octavia was pregnant. Octavia, so pure and lady-like, with her idealistic standards! What a sell-out if she got there first. Who would have supposed it – and how on earth did she dare?

Chapter 29

There was a gap of more than three weeks before another letter came from Hugo. Yet it had been written within two days of his previous letter, just before he left Luang Prabang for his work in the mountain villages. It appeared to have been tampered with. But then, it had travelled an awfully long way. Her family would hardly be likely to nose into her private mail. Octavia dismissed her feeling of uneasisness.

Poor Isabel. She thought, not having a Hugo. She had Nicholas, but of course that wouldn't last. Either Nicholas would get bored of Isabel's clamorous demands for sympathy – or he'd provide it; and then Isabel would get bored with him. In the privacy of Miss Carpenter's little office, Octavia returned to Hugo's letter, convincing herself of its cheerfulness.

'Luang Prabang must surely be my favourite place in the world. Nothing here has changed, thank heaven. It has a timeless peace that's beyond description. I find myself wishing over and over again that you were here. I can almost imagine you are, I carry such a strong sense of you around with me. That's the power of your absence at work in these surroundings. All is gracious and graceful and I'm serious when I say it's how I think of you. The temples have an unostentatious beauty like the women, who must be amongst the loveliest in the world. Everything is unhurried. There's a lot of laughter, and one is made to feel entirely welcome. Today I watched groups of Meo appearing in the market with quantities of fresh produce, the children decked out in their heavy silver necklets and bracelets, even toddlers, wearing short black jackets and round hats and not much else. I've made contact with a party from the village I was in last January and should be setting out with them tomorrow.

'Do keep the letters coming. Send them care of the Embassy in Vientiane and if they can't forward them I'll have the Max

Fortune saga in book form when I come back. I told you he was impossible and am not surprised he's getting worse. Don't add to your problems by worrying about my safety. Serious danger is minimal and believe me, I'm not looking for unnecessary trouble. Verifying last year's research data is my only concern.'

Trouble. The very word made Octavia freeze. Perhaps Muth's superstition was infectious. It had become vital not to take anything for granted, not to tempt providence, not to celebrate yet. Hugo seemed to be recovering from an illness. All she could do was keep very calm, very quiet. Not upset the balance. She was beginning to put a sensational, even a morbid interpretation on Hugo's preference for keeping their engagement secret. He was playing safe too, unsure if he'd come back alive.

Hearing voices in the passage, Octavia began typing letters for Miss Carpenter. She'd finished them and started a sheet of film data when the voices returned, considerably raised now. Then Max Fortune came in abruptly and told her that Isabel was unwell and had had to go home. Since it was Norah's day off and Miss Carpenter had agreed, would she please come at once. Reluctantly, with a sense of her friend's betrayal, Octavia followed him.

Fortune was chairing a meeting at half-past three. She might need to take shorthand notes, he said. Meanwhile, a letter to his squash coach must catch the next post. Octavia wasted precious minutes trying to make out this letter. Then she swallowed her pride and rang Norah, who informed her that she was in the middle of making pastry. The voice was remote and impatient. Octavia explained the trouble. Norah mentioned a radio programme she'd been obliged to switch off. Octavia repeated her request and was told to try the folder on Relaxtion. In the Personal Section. Then Norah hung up and Octavia went in search.

There were folders for all the members of Fortune's family, albums of photographs and an interior decoration scheme for his house in Mayfair. But no folder for Relaxtion. She cried aloud, 'Norah's probably got it with her!' She then imagined Isabel stowing it in the wrong place. She felt furious with them both, and wanted to return to her room and think about Hugo. Unless she held him constantly in her thoughts he might suffer the consequences . . .

She was confronted by her icy employer. He was in a bad

mood that morning. He wanted to know what Norah had written to Mr Rochester the previous week, and whether there was a note of his business address. Octavia thought how petty he sounded.

'Do you not know where anything is? I expected you to familiar with API files long ago.'

That pulled her up. 'Of course I know where things are,' she said. 'I'll bring the folder at once.'

He banged out of the room. She went to fetch the John Rochester folder, only to find that it had disappeared. She searched for it on Isabel's desk and amongst the other folders. No trace. There was nothing for it. She knocked on Fortune's door and confessed.

'That's ridiculous!' He lifted his palms. 'You've had all summer to master the filing. Don't tell me you girls are making MORE work for everyone?'

Octavia glared at him and said, 'I understand the filing system, Max. But the John Rochester folder is missing. Lots of folders are in a mess.'

'Then you presumably made them so. Norah is meticulous with my papers. I suggest you and the other girl go through them with her again the moment she's back. I can't have my time wasted. I shall have to speak to Norah. Please ring her now.'

It was an ordeal waiting for Norah to answer. When at last she did, Octavia thrust the receiver at Fortune so he could bear the brunt of her wrath. She could detect a change in Norah's tone from where she stood. Fortune hung up. He marched over to Norah's desk and discovered a file tucked into one of its bottom drawers. He snatched it out and the left the room without another glance.

Octavia forgot the squash coach letter and applied herself to the others. Her mind was clogged with unresolved duties and questions. She thought, I need never come in here again.

She was fetched for the meeting. By this time Fortune could hardly bring himself to speak to her. She was confronted by four other men. They sat in an informal crescent around a long gilt coffee table, and balefully watched her find a chair. Several moments elapsed before they all ceased to look furtively in her direction. She wondered if Fortune had briefed them on his new secretary, so deceptively harmless, so destructive.

The meeting was unintelligible. The men employed a technical vocabulary which was unfamiliar to Octavia. They seemed to revel in digressions. Fortune ignored her, giving no hint as to which parts of the discussion she was to record and which to ignore. When she concentrated on the talk she fell behind with her notes. When she concentrated on the notes they lacked logic. She suspected her attendance was a punishment to keep her from her desk.

As she flicked over the page of her short-hand book in an effort to keep up, Fortune told her to fetch his previous year's diary. Forcing herself to appear relaxed, she rose. He was staring at his folded hands, his expression blank. His visitors watched with interest as she went to the door. She knew she'd find no diary.

There was no sound while she was gone.

She searched Norah's desk, then all the desk drawers and the dusty top shelves. The silence endured, and she went back.

'Yes?' said Fortune.

'I should have asked you where the old diaries are kept.' Octavia wanted to bring menace to bear, but two of the jury were smiling slightly at each other.

'Oh, for heaven's sake!' Fortune exclaimed. He got up and pushed into her room. If he'd hoped to make a bigger fool of her in front of his colleagues he had succeeded. But her shame was contaminating him. She felt they made an entertaining duo. He flung an arm towards the doorway and hissed, 'People will think I employ nitwits here.'

He began to raid the room for his diary while she perched on her desk in defiance. She said, 'Norah's tuition didn't cover old diaries.'

That brought him over to her. He was white with anger. He shut the communicating door. He said, 'I must have been out of my senses to take you on. You've been nothing but a nuisance since you arrived. It's as well Norah is away so I see you in your true light. Miss Carpenter must be a saint.'

'True light!' Octavia retorted. 'Do you think this has been a fair test? How can I do two people's work in a disorganized office, and spend time on private letters?'

'Be quiet!' shouted Fortune. 'You have caused chaos for me. I've a good mind to dismiss you.' Vanishing into his room, he banged the door.

Octavia remembered trying to comfort Isabel after a fraught

morning, speaking in a way she now thought rather glib: 'Don't worry. Max isn't bad at heart. He'll get over it.'

Then she remembered the urgent letter to the squash coach. She sat at her desk and stared at the typewriter.

The door opened. Fortune was back. 'I shall check whether Miss Carpenter is satisfied with your work. I've seen you behave as if this was a holiday home. A Butlin's Camp perhaps! You're here to fill in, as you see it, before going to the Foreign Office. But I intend to warn them. Maybe Miss Carpenter has given you a positive reference. But I'll tell them to have nothing to do with you!'

He disappeared. Octavia smiled smugly to herself. She'd received a letter of acceptance from the Foreign Office that morning. If only Hugo were there. If she could only talk to him on the phone, the way Isabel was always talking to Nicholas.

At that moment the telephone rang.

An urgent telegram. Concerning a Mr Hugo Talbot.

Octavia grew icy with fear. Lily Falange. Death in the family. She and Hugo should never have got engaged. Moving into their family circle, he'd signed his death warrant.

Something about flight details. British Oversea Airways. Heathrow. An arrival time and a date, which Octavia had to have repeated. She checked it again.

Hugo would be back next day.

Chapter 30

Having left instructions with the porter as to where he could be found, Hugo walked down the hall of his Club and into the pleasant library which overlooked gardens at the back. He stood at the windows. A green outlook. Trees and lawns, with Carlton Terrace beyond. The sun was shining. To Hugo it was unreal. For him reality was still the primitive, empty countryside of Northern Laos, near the border with Vietnam; where he'd been so shaken by what he'd seen. Not the horror of war – yet. But the build-up. It was one thing to condone American policy. Quite another to approve their methods. Patience was needed. Minimum force, not the full might of US power.

A voice behind him said, 'Shouldn't you be writing that report?'

Hugo swung round. James, confound him! This was indeed like being back in Laos, with CIA agents watching one's every move. 'My dear James! A galling sense of prep school revisited comes over me. 'Where is that essay? Why hasn't it been handed in?''

'On the contrary. I delight in the informality of your schoolboy world. I encourage it. Your essay will just appear one day – with its usual panache, I'm sure, and – as usual – headed by an erudite Laotian proverb.' Hugo remaining silent, he added, 'Are you lunching here?'

'Yes. With a friend.'

'Ah! Anyone I know?'

'It's Octavia Ransome's brother. Not someone you know – or would want to know.'

'How can you be so sure? Is he attractive, like his sister?'

'He's a very normal young man. Of no interest to you whatever.'

Facing down James's whimsical smile, Hugo continued brusquely, 'I know what you think of Octavia, James. But

114

I've become very fond of her. Her letters to me in Laos were a something of a life-line. Now I feel a bit concerned about her.'

'That's stretching credulity a bit far, Hugo. You're 'concerned' about the sister, so you invite the brother to lunch.'

'I wish you'd be serious, James. The fact is, I'm applying my training as a CIA operative. I'm using the brother to get my bearings on the sister.'

'It's clear how serious YOU'VE become, Hugo. I have your interests at heart, you know. But first things first. Concentrate on that report. I know the job is done, and that your written account is a mere formality. But it will be read – widely, I hope. And then, in certain circles, I will again be credited with the excellence of my little band of brothers.'

'You'll have your report this evening, James. I'm sorry it wasn't written the day before yesterday – but the fact is, this particular little brother is feeling kinda screwed up. Both about what he was let in for . . . and about US policy. To be absolutely frank with you, I resent the way the montagnards are being manipulated. It's indefensible. Arming the Meos is typical of Western short sightedness. The only outcome will be a terrible refugee problem along the Mekong.'

'If there's any hint of that in your report, I'll suppress it. In your own interests, Hugo. A hard, simplistic focus please. Remember our white-kneed, blue-eyed readers in the Pentagon. Mission accomplished. Talbot triumphs again. A Laotian proverb or two. End of story.' James laid a hand on Hugo's shoulder. 'And do bring some brutality to bear on poor Miss Ransome. She's very young. You're deluding yourself over her. You're a professional, so committed to that academic reputation of yours that you seriously thought you could hang on after completing your mission for us. With Pathet Lao activity less than five miles away! Thank God you understood the danger.'

James paused, wanting to develop his theme, deciding this was not the place or time. He patted the handkerchief in his breast pocket. 'Referring to your academic reputation,' he went on, 'I mean it when I say it enhances mine. That girl wouldn't give you the space you need. If it's selling one's soul we're talking about, she's the gold-plated way of doing it. You'd be kissing goodbye to the Travellers and a comfortable bachelor life-style. You just need a break Hugo, after what you've been through.'

Outside the Club, Nicholas was thinking, So this is it! Pretty awesome ...

Turning his back on Pall Mall, he entered the building. He was at once met with the porter's discreet challenge and, giving his name and Hugo's, was led along the hall and shown into the library. 'I'm afraid I'm a bit late,' he said, taken aback by the presence of James and a crowd of strangers who came into the room after him.

Hugo introduced them, and James gave the young guest his most exclusive attention. On the tall side. Attractive face. Honey blond hair. James's expression seemed to say, You're exactly what I expected. And more.

It was Nicholas he now patted on the shoulder. 'Hugo in his impetuously generous way has been coaxing me to join you for lunch. But it's back to the shop, alas. I hope we can meet on some other occasion.' He walked Hugo to the door murmuring, 'I feel rudely excluded. By you, of all people. I look on you as that rare entity Hugo, a pal as well as a colleague.'

He ambled away. But when Hugo invited Nicholas to follow him to the central staircase he was aware of James lurking near the porter's lodge, watching their ascent.

Skirting the large oval of the central table, they went to one reserved for them against the wall. Nicholas was surprised by how busy the Club was and how loudly the convivial babble filled the dining room. He took his seat with youthful dignity, pink at the pleasure of seeing Hugo again in such special circumstances. Hugo himself didn't look well. There was an esoteric reserve to his manner, a jadedness of skin, which Nicholas only gradually noticed.

'It's quite a time since I was last in this room,' Hugo said. 'Normally we'd sit at the centre table and I'd introduced you to some of the members. But I see our MP for Kemp Town looking expectantly in this direction. I'd rather preserve our privacy today.'

Nicholas was eager to hear from Hugo how his trip had gone and what the fruits of his excursions would be. Hugo supplied him with bland descriptions of data for lectures, and referred to stacks of photographs all needing to be put into order. Once more the magical names rolled out. Ban Houei Sai. Muong Neua. The Plain of Jars. From the time he first heard it mentioned, Nicholas had determined to go to the Plain of Jars. He twiddled his cufflinks. 'Have you any more travelling in the offing? Next year I mean – or in the near future?' He warily cleared his throat.

Hugo stretched his legs. 'Very little idea where I shall be. Those decisions rest with SOAS. And other incidentals conspire.'

Incidentals, thought Nicholas. Like marriage? It was at that moment he realized how strained Hugo looked.

'And what have you been doing lately? I'm informed that tea has gone up in price. Can you rationalise that calamity?'

'Oh well, yes.' Nicholas stretched his feet to within an inch of Hugo's. He drew breath. But their waiter came over and the moment passed.

Hugo sealed the interruption. 'How do you find Octavia at the moment? I was a little concerned to see she'd lost weight. What's the state of her morale?'

'I think she realized from your letters this hasn't been an easy trip. The one describing your illness upset her a lot.'

'I didn't describe it, surely? I kept quiet about it. Or meant to.'

'She sensed something was wrong. You made that much obvious.'

'Are you telling me you read it?' Hugo frowned. It was one thing to presume the interference of a hostile intelligence service. Quite another where your correspondent's brother was concerned.

Nicholas coloured. 'It was actually Isabel who told me.'

'Octavia's been showing my letters to Isabel? So they're common knowledge all over the API?'

'Goodness, no. Of course not. It was just a letter Isabel found lying about and glanced at. Yes, the API crowd are keen for news of you. But it isn't the happy-go-lucky place you remember. There was a fair amount of stress while you were away, in fact. I expect Octavia's told you about that.'

'Give me your version.'

Nicholas launched into an account of the confrontation with Fortune. He lingered so long over Isabel's actions and reactions that Hugo grew restive. He said, 'I gathered from what Octavia wrote that what was amusing became a bit less so. Doesn't surprise me that Max Fortune flipped, he always had a short fuse. But what do you mean, the API is keen for my news? Define news for me.'

'Your adventures; and then your coming back so unexpectedly. Don't worry Hugo, Isabel's the only one to know of the engagement – and she's terribly discreet.'

'And what about your mother? She must have got wind of this 'engagement' by now?'

'Mother's fairly oblivious, as usual.' There was a pause, while Hugo decided to make contact with Roweena without delay. He was tempted to ring her from the Club as soon as Nicholas had left. On second thoughts, he'd sleep on it.

'You mentioned Vivian in one of your letters.' Nicholas jibbed, apprehensively. 'She was your ex-wife, I suppose? I hope you don't mind my asking.'

'Yes, you're right.' Hugo sighed. 'That was my ex-wife.' There was another pause. He thought of the espionage team scrutinizing his letters: saucy Isabel, staid Nicholas. A disconcerting combination. Perhaps he should put in a word for them with James.

Nicholas tried again. 'What can I tell Tavia about meeting you?'

'I'd be grateful if you'd quietly emphasise the stress I've been under myself, and the priority I must give to sorting out my material. But keep it low key. She's anyway inclined to fret about danger – and my health. Don't get excited about our engagement either, there's a good chap. We're not ready to announce it yet. Too much to work out.'

He took a sip of wine, opening his mouth slightly and breathing in before rolling it round his palate, rather as Nicholas was used to seeing tea tasted. Now he found the procedure oddly disturbing.

Hugo went on, 'You know, another factor has been political developments out there. The West has seen to it that people with money and power have their Mercedes cars and big colonial houses. All the luxuries for which they're so greedy – and you can imagine the result. The indigenous culture is threatened. People in the sticks have scarcely more than primitive ploughs for their buffalo, and baskets for winnowing rice. Class distinctions are evolving that weren't there before.' He motioned with his glass. 'What d'you think of the Club claret?'

'I like it enormously.' Nicholas took a healthy draught. His host seemed to be regarding him with faintly hostile abstraction.

'Since you're so familiar with my private correspondence Nicholas, you'll perhaps not be embarrassed if I extol the Lao girls to you. Especially in Luang Prabang. They're exquisite. Infinitely receptive and anxious to please. Feminine I suppose I mean. In a contradictory way they reminded me of Octavia. Well, you'll have read about that too, of course. No doubt to the accompaniment of Isabel's merry laughter. Octavia has a certain grace – if not a tendency to submission. A quality of freshness one hesitates to touch.' He cleared his throat. 'I may have told you this before,' he went on, 'but Lao weaving is strongly localized in character. Not so much fashion, but status. Aristocratic families jealously guard their secrets. The Luang Prabang silk skirt, or sinh, features a pattern of ornaments, usually in gold thread. It isn't only peasants who work the handlooms either. The nobility pass their skills down from mother to daughter. Luang Prabang ornamentation is inserted, not woven. It's like embroidery, but integral to the pattern. I can't tell you how lovely and subtle the effect is, and how upset I am to see that wonderful civilisation being destroyed.'

Nicholas sat forward, prepared to hear more, but disturbed at the abrupt way Hugo was now talking, and his emphasis on loss of culture over human life. He'd guaranteed himself an hour and a half in this agreeable ambiance. He'd made arrangements at his office in the City. But the tension in his host's manner had become worrying ; and he was aware that the dining room was steadily emptying.

Hugo glanced at his watch. 'I have to be at a meeting in Portland Place by two fifteen. Better go. I imagine you ought to be moving too.'

Nicholas felt suddenly crestfallen. He had another forty minutes in hand. Perhaps he'd walk up into St James's and buy something for Isabel.

Chapter 31

The phone on Octavia's desk rang. She'd been hoping Hugo would telephone and at last he had.

'Hello darling. Busy?'

'Not too busy. Why? Where are you?'

'The Albany. I'm sitting at James's desk surrounded by correspondence all demanding attention. There's a granary loaf and some pate in the kitchen. Can you come round?'

Oh, for the days when Hugo would drop in and casually walk her out to Green Park, or up Regent Street, or over to Carlton Terrace and the Duke of York Steps; when they both seemed to have all the time in the world. But it was nonetheless Hugo, wanting her to go to him. She finished typing an envelope, tidied her desk and hurried out. Liz glanced up briefly. A subversive smile – but because of the stricter office policy there was no exchange of banter. Octavia experienced an excited dread. She rapidly rounded the corner by Swann and Edgars and almost ran down Piccadilly and into the Albany forecourt.

Hugo opened the door to her and at the same time opened his arms. He held her very close and she was instantly full of joy, all anxiety erased as if it had never been. One arm still around her, they went to the kitchen where he'd been preparing plates of bread spread with pate.

'Make some coffee,' he instructed her, taking a new box of Florentines from a cupboard.

Only when they were in James's drawing room did an insidious dissatisfaction creep back into Octavia's mind. Hugo sat himself at the desk, with his lunch before him. She had to pull up a chair to be near.

'I can't believe we're here, together,' she said, starting a sandwich with gusto. 'How are you, darling Hugo, now you're really back?' She gazed into his face. She'd been concerned at what Nicholas had told her of his lunch at the Travellers: Hugo's suspicion that everyone at API would be discussing his business behind his back, and the careful way Nicholas had described Hugo as looking and sounding strained. 'Are you jaundiced?'

'Am I?' He was addressing his food, not facing her. 'I think I'm pretty well recovered. Must keep off alcohol for a while. Not indulge in rich goodies.'

She exclaimed, 'But Hugo, that's ridiculous! You're tucking into pate and butter now – and what about those Florentines you've got lined up?'

'Too bad. I'll stint myself tomorrow.'

Her spirit was roused in that light moment of confrontation. His averted face, the stubborn pleasure in what might damage his liver, ignited antagonism. 'Was it useful meeting Nicky yesterday?' she asked in as normal a tone as she could muster.

'Not in the least useful.' He licked pate off a finger.

'Then you could just as easily have met me for lunch.'

'Darling, I felt I ought to fit Nicky in while I could. You can't imagine what a slog it is, completing all the donkey work that follows a tour abroad; and how important it is to get it right. A great deal hangs on what further research projects come out of it, and how much reclame my lectures attract.'

'I understand that perfectly.' Octavia picked up a piece of bread and put it down again. 'You've told me several times. But you don't realize how immensely privileged your work is to engage SO much of your attention.' It was a weakness, she knew, letting emotion lure her into sarcasm.

It wasn't unlike their walks on the Downs, he was thinking. With a surplus of enthusiasm and energy, she'd always been one step ahead. She'd gone right in front now, way past the limit he'd set himself. She had no right to force herself on him in this way. He had it in him to discipline her, and she might as well know it. He could very easily demonstrate his authority over her. Control her perceptions and her expectations.

Watching him polish off the bread and reach for a Florentine, Octavia felt rejected and snubbed. He was punishing her because she loved him, and was loyal.

'I do dislike being a nuisance to you,' she said, standing and going to a low table covered with boxes of transparencies.

She crouched down to examine them. 'You make me feel like a tiresome brat. No doubt it's not very adult being unable to cope with pressures of work and a disinterested fiancé at the same time.' Still that note of sarcasm. But it released so much tension.

He managed a tight laugh. 'You're a bully, you know. I realized that some time ago.' He took another Florentine. 'It was a mistake to let Isabel trumpet our engagement round the API. These things take time, especially when there are separations.'

'She didn't trumpet it round. And nor did I. People draw their own conclusions.'

'That's Amelia Sedley talk. Positively anachronistic, from a star of the sixties culture.'

'Don't call me Amelia Sedley, I'm tired of it. You're spoiling a good book and making a fool of me. In the same way you've made a fool of me with Muth, I'm beginning to suspect.'

'I've told you before that I think your mother's probably more emancipated than you are. You worry too much about niceties that strike me as rather bourgeois. I'm surprised. You revealed such a sophisticated side that night at the Congreve. I really admired your whole-hearted grasp of its strategy and wit.'

'Well, if being engaged is all strategy and wit, I'm not sure I care about it.'

'You completely miss the point. I'm disappointed in you Octavia.'

She threw him a chilly glance. 'It would have been nice if you'd called for me at the office, instead of summoning me to your friend's apartment.'

'My dear girl, I was under the impression you worked behind an iron curtain now. I should hate to compromise you further in Max Fortune's baleful eyes.'

So that was all the sympathy API's one-time hero was prepared to offer! Octavia flung a full box of transparencies over the couch.

Hugo rose, collected the contents and shut his box grimly in a drawer of the desk. 'For God's sake don't meddle with those. Now listen. We'll make a proper announcement and follow it up with celebration drinks, speeches, the lot. But you must allow me to have a say in how and when we do it.'

He offered her the Florentines, helped himself to another and sat in an armchair. 'Alternatively, we could just bugger off. Not invite anybody. Simply choose a date and get married. No fuss.'

'Not having to show the slightest consideration for anyone else. And no expense.'

He leaned over and touched her with a rigid forefinger so that it hurt. 'Now wait a minute. You're rather overdoing the cynicism. It cheapens what you have to say; and you'll regret it later.'

'You're as bad as Mother. What she doesn't approve of, she ignores. You're exactly the same.'

A wave of distaste both for Roweena and Octavia flooded him. Deluded into believing he'd needed them, and having shared to an extent in their dream world, he was now being criticized as a member of it. 'I hope you're keeping an eye on the time,' he said. 'You don't want to be out of a job.' He saw a stony expression cross her face. In contravention of his orders, she was peering at transparencies from another box. It was the set which featured the Kha tribespeople. She tipped them in a heap saying, 'I don't really know you at all.'

'Indeed.' Hugo went back to the desk. His expression became so acid that she was chilled. He took up his fountain pen and pulled over a sheet of paper.

It was terrible to be slighted in the middle of a quarrel, left high and dry with all her anger alive and nothing concluded. Marriage wouldn't bring security. There would always be a fear of losing or disliking him. She said in a tight voice, 'Hugo.'

He didn't bother to look up but said, 'I'm writing to a friend. Please be quiet for a while.' In fact he was writing the overdue report on his Xiengkhouang mission. His anger was now directed on himself.

'Hugo!'

'Please be quiet!'

'I won't be quiet. We're discussing our engagement and wedding.' She felt cold even while her blood was rapidly heating.

'What a cheek you've got. Constant reminders that you're not a child only reinforce your immaturity, by the way.'

'How can you be so horrible! You obviously don't care a jot about our future.'

'No,' said Hugo,' at this moment I don't. I only wish to communicate with an adult.' He pretended to apply himself to this end, and she stood up. It was difficult to know what to do. She'd been prepared to ring Miss Carpenter from the Albany and say she had a headache and couldn't return for the afternoon.

'I'm sorry to interrupt you, but please remember you're under no obligations. Since you're so indifferent, I'd be happy to call everything off. I'll marry someone my age.'

She went to the door. Hugo flung down his pen and swept over to her. He caught her elbow and forced her on to the couch. 'Now wait a minute,' he said through his teeth. 'I'm not letting that sort of talk go unanswered.' His forehead was like damp wax, his mouth turning down as if he, too, was curbing tears. She wilted under his grip and he squeezed her to provoke some response. 'Well?'

'Well,' she repeated, improvising wildly, 'I said I don't expect you to marry me. You have other women in the wings. I don't want to cramp your style.'

His small mouth twitched with contempt. He was tempted to take her at her word and ditch her, guilty for wanting to, yet lacking the courage. He searched her face without affection, amazed that she could speak like that. She met his look bravely, knowing she had hurt him and sure he would never forget.

'My instincts were right. I'll have to consider our next move.'

Dismay showed on her face. She began, 'What instincts?' Her head was aching.

'Yes.' His tone was laconic. He clapped his hand over her knee. It was quite simple to seem all-wise, all-powerful, and get away with it. 'I shall decide. Now don't interfere Octavia, because it's going to make me very angry again.'

Her eye in profile, a blue half-sphere; the rounded cheek and chin. 'I shall want to see your mother.'

'When?' she demanded, in denial that they were actually together, and she full of dislike.

'Possibly one evening during the week. And please tell Nicholas he can mind his own business.'

In the early days, they'd spent time in London, and the weekends in Sussex. Now their plans were to be apart.

Hugo turned his back on her. 'If you've any affection left for me darling Octavia, you'll trot back to Golden Square and let me finish my work.'

Chapter 32

Hugo watched. Parking was not her forte. She completed the final run backwards, struck the kerb with a flourish, and climbed out on to the road. She was wearing a dazzling cloche hat. Now she appeared to be raiding her handbag for something. A party of people came noisily past, knocking her elbows, looking through her. But Hugo had eyes for no-one else. What was that coat she was wearing? A nameless fur, he thought, staring furtively from his window.

'Hugo dear . . . I feared I'd lost my wallet for a moment.'

He drew her through the outer front door of his flat. Of course there'd been some muddle, some drama. Roweena was coming into splendid focus, banishing his self-absorption at long last.

She said, 'Well, you wretched man, aren't you going to embrace me? I need rejuvenating! I feel a hundred years old today.'

Automatically, he embraced her. She pulled free almost at once. 'Just as well we're meeting here, rather than my gadding up to Town. I'm a stranger in London now, and I've probably forgotten how imposing a West End address can be. Heaven knows what I'd have worn for Albany.'

'Nothing special, I assure you. I must say Roweena, you look splendid. I saw you arriving, and thought your hat was a knockout.'

'The power of positive thinking. Yes, this is a much nicer plan. I imagine Albany's full of clergymen and government ministers. All celibate. Silly, the fancies one has about places. This is lovely! It has the feel of family still. Generations of Talbots. I've been most curious to see you against your background.'

'Well now you know. It's not at all grand. But it suits my life-style. The number of generations, by the way, is two. My parents, who retired here, and me.'

'The scale of these rooms is very pleasant. These terraces seem to wear their period like good clothes – elegantly. But the shabby streets you see around, the run-down squares, they depress one rather. Gilbert wouldn't have believed Britain could become so scruffy.'

Hugo handed her a glass of sherry. 'I'm lucky. I have good views from both ends of the flat. My car hasn't been stolen – yet. I can reach the sea in seven minutes.'

Roweena was taking in all the details of the room. She asked about the pieces of Laotian silk displayed on various surfaces and the more splendid tribal piece hanging on the wall. There was also a tribal sword which she liked. Presently she went to his bathroom. He heard her opening doors. They were a snoopy lot, the Ransomes.

'You're a very tidy man,' she accused him, coming back. 'Do you have someone who keeps you straight?'

'What makes you suppose I need anyone to keep me straight, as you put it? Perhaps I'm just boringly organised. Isn't that something of a virtue?'

'You get ten out of ten all round. I'm dreadfully chaotic, I know it. This room now – it's like a museum. Delightful – but not homely. You need to be tidy in your work, I daresay?'

'Next time I'll make a hearty mess to welcome you. Of course, there's no great merit in being tidy when one lives alone. I don't even have a cat to disrupt things.'

'Tell me Hugo, what are the pictures in your bedroom? Octavia describes pictures in Mr Wedge's flat, and I imagine those are similar?'

'They are temple rubbings. The figures are dancers and musicians.'

'How interesting. Now, would they be tourist booty, or are they very old and valuable?'

'Those have no particular value. They're available everywhere to tourists. But some of the items James has are in a very different category.'

'I wonder how he finds them. It must be a help, having your advice. Do you bring them back for his collection? Most people wouldn't know where to go and what to buy. I suppose he's an expert too?'

Hugo took a slow sip of sherry. 'I'm responsible for bringing back a number of very rare pieces, as a matter of fact. It goes against the grain to remove some of them, but the temples need the money. James is a connoisseur, so his treasures are appreciated. And protected from neglect.'

Roweena set her glass down with emphasis. 'I don't think you should endorse that sort of practice. Even for a friend. He struck me as a self-indulgent person, your Mr Wedge. But who am I to preach? I'm talking badly out of turn.'

'Not a bit. What you say is valid – though quite honestly only up to a point. It was Octavia's reaction too. Blame me, not poor old James. He's less self-indulgent than you think.'

'He's amusing. But he's not the sort of person I could trust. You see – I tell you any nonsense that occurs to me. It's as if we've been friends for years. That's the difference. I'd be very much more reticent with him and never feel I knew him. He wouldn't be generous with his friendship.'

It was generous of her, Hugo said ten minutes later, to drive them to the restaurant off the Old Steine. 'Don't thank me too soon,' she warned. 'This isn't anyone's car, remember. It's mine.'

She parked near the Chinese restaurant where he'd taken Octavia on their first outing. Where they'd had lunch, and he'd shown her how to hold chopsticks, and she had transformed him into someone different. They sat where Hugo had sat before. Roweena tossed off her hat and they studied the enormous menu.

'Perhaps if I sit beside you it might be easier,' Hugo murmured. He squeezed on to the plush seat with the menu between them and they read through the choices. Then there was some fun about their waiter, who brought the Chinese tea. 'He's like a naval officer trying to foxtrot,' Hugo whispered. 'A partner worthy of your talent. I know you shone on the dance floor with Gilbert.'

She didn't catch what he'd said, and leaned clumsily near to hear him repeat it, which reluctantly he did. The remark struck him as even more crass the second time, and there she was, fitting him fold for fold as he spoke, then chuckling heartily, entering into the spirit of talking at random with nothing to lose.

He told her about API, and the little he knew of life at Buckland Crescent. He assumed Octavia didn't relate quite all the harmless details which might be dear to a mother's heart.

Octavia! Was the man obsessed with her? Roweena wondered. 'Are you obsessed with Octavia?'

'Heavens. I hope not. But that isn't to say I'm not fond of her.'

'Oh my dear,' Roweena said. 'You told me so before. Don't you remember, you once spent a whole afternoon telling me just that! The day I felt so ill.'

As she toyed with her chopsticks, Hugo laid a hand on hers. Glancing into her face, he made the observation that eating in China was very different from having a sociable meal in the West. Nowadays it was quite common to see beer being served, or even a brandy bottle on the table.

'Good gracious yes,' Roweena cut in. 'When we were stationed at Singapore after the war, that was very much the custom. Brandy certainly – but gin used to feature as much. Gilbert swore gin cleaned the palette and sharpened the appetite better than anything. And I mean several measures, not just a splash.'

Somewhat deflated, Hugo leaned back. 'You won't need advice on how to handle chopsticks then.' He called to the waiter to bring a couple of brandies forthwith.

'Don't imagine it was Raffles we patronized all the time, either,' Roweena said. She held up her glass. 'Not a bit of it! Gilbert used to take me to Bugis Street. Never mind the riffraff, the prostitutes and what have you. To tell the truth, we'd spot Gilbert's ratings vanishing into the most insalubrious doorways, and turn the proverbial blind eye! Oh yes, I adored life in Singapore.'

Their dishes started to arrive on the table. Hugo leaned over and helped her to a bed of rice, some chicken with almonds and ginger, some noodles. He helped himself and, beginning to eat, watched her hands. She was using the chopsticks with commendable skill. She selected a slippery mushroom and dropped it in his bowl.

He said, 'Now that has to be showing off!'

She was pleased and amused. Then it was her turn to peer closely at him. 'D'you know, I think you're a very secretive man?'

'I don't think I'm secretive.' Hugo concentrated on his heaped bowl. He wondered what was coming, having grown used to compliments which turned out to be brickbats.

'You have a thousand and one secrets, collected from all corners of the globe. I'm positive. It was borne in on me again in the car, what a good listener you are; but how little of yourself you give away.'

'That's chastening, coming from you.'

'Coming from me?'

'Yes. I've done nothing but push myself forward and trespass on your kind nature ever since we met. Not very reticent behaviour, surely?'

'Oh, don't imagine I mind. Secretive men are the most interesting. I used to think that dozens of years ago, when I was quite a young thing. I believe I told Gilbert once that I wished he had a few secrets. Young women like to believe their husbands are a bit wicked.'

Hugo was astonished. This, after the trauma of Planchette! She seemed to have forgotten it completely. 'I doubt if all young women would agree with you.'

'Perhaps not. But to be far from secret with you Hugo, my husband used to bore me a little. I'd have given my ears to learn he was having an affair with someone. Isn't that a shocking confession?'

Hugo assumed she was compensating for a memory that shamed her. In her youth maybe she'd wanted a vagrant husband. How different was the mother from the daughter. 'You look enchanting in that deep red,' he heard himself say, not eloquently but sincerely.

She chuckled. 'Oh Hugo – no wonder Octavia is attached to you, if you flatter her as well.'

'That,' he replied, 'is not very flattering to me.'

'No. I'm not much good at compliments. But I'll tell you one thing. It was a chance meeting at the Brighton barrier that brought us all together, and you've bucked up our poor lives no end. Nicholas would say so too.'

He asked, 'Forgive me if this sounds inquisitive, but have you ever considered remarrying?' He replenished her bowl, aware of the heavy masculine ring on a finger of her right hand. On the fourth finger of her left hand she wore no ring at all.

'No,' came the immediate reply. 'No. Never for one instant. I'm very content as I am.' But she said as an after-thought, 'He did take mistresses latterly, you know. I'm sure of it; and by then I really did care a bit.' She threw him an appealing glance. 'But you've heard all that, of course.'

'I was married, and it didn't work out.'

'I'm very sorry my dear. I can't think you were a quarrelsome man.'

'No. Not quarrelsome. But I was selfish – still am. And so was she.' He inclined closer to her and tapped her finger. 'What a handsome ring, Roweena!' Leaving his hand on hers, he added wistfully, before the waiter could disturb them, 'I felt guilty about the failure of my marriage. So guilty that I invented a woman to compensate for failure, someone called Diana to justify the mess I'd made. I told my wife about her. She was pure invention!'

Hugo watched a party of what he took to be a mix of English and Chinese fill the next table. Then he added, taking her hand again and playing with her ring, 'There, how's that for a secret? Now you know one of them, at any rate.'

'Diana,' Roweena said, her head on one side. 'Diana. That's a pretty name. It was on my short list for Nicholas. I wonder why you called her Diana? But of course – Diana the Chaste.'

'Or Diana of the Chase.' Hugo called for more brandy. 'It was a foolish attempt to bolster my morale. I say I felt guilty over the failure of our marriage. But it was more bitterness than guilt, I realize now. She resented my work, my love of French Indochina, and I thought her very selfish. This walk into Xiengkhouang, for example. It was marvelous, despite the fact it took longer than I'd expected, and my American anthropologist turned out to be less than a soul mate. But I loved the time spent sitting with the village people, with their children, and at improvised clinics. Vivian would have been bored, and fussed about sanitation and mosquitoes. Some of these tribes don't understand the wheel but have a sophisticated social hierarchy. That kind of paradox meant nothing to Vivian. With her in tow my success and even my safety would have been at risk.'

'You make her sound rather unreasonable. But what lack of judgment on your part, Hugo! Perhaps, like me, you aren't very good at weighing up character.'

'I'm sure I could have taken Octavia with me. Going for long walks on the Sussex Downs with her is enough to convince me of it. I even doubt if we'd ever quarrel.' His mind flashed to the scene in the Albany. 'Not seriously, anyway.'

'There! That's lack of judgment again. Of course you would! She can be terribly obstinate and difficult. Usually in innocence,

I grant you.'

Hugo didn't answer. He was reflecting on how lucky he'd been to get free from Vivian, the cunning he'd shown in waiting for her to make the first move. He'd known before she asked him for a divorce that the other man was a rotter.

'Yes, it was very painful. Emasculating,' he muttered.

Seeing Roweena's surprised expression he added, 'It was a homeopath Vivian went off with. He made her pregnant. I knew it wouldn't work. But I was well out of it.' Roweena's surprise growing, he was conscious of revealing a more unpleasant side of himself than he'd intended. He drained the last drop of brandy from his glass. 'Those were the bad days. I suppose I have more blessings to count now than I deserve.'

Chapter 33

Walking back to the car, Roweena took Hugo's arm. She said, 'Have you seen your friend Guy Beamish lately? He was rather a dear, wasn't he?'

So she remembered him – and his name. He must have impressed her. 'Not lately. But he continues to support the Theatre Royal. An amusing fellow. But not the marrying kind, if you know what I mean.'

'Oh marriage!' she said. 'You and I have had enough of marriage.'

She stopped suddenly and so did he.

'I don't think I can drive,' she said. 'My head isn't clear. Nothing to do with the brandy. I'm not the least bit tipsy. I felt dizzy leaving the restaurant – but I tried to ignore it.'

'You really don't feel up to driving?'

'I'm afraid I might prang us if I drove.'

They'd come to the Morris and Roweena touched it affectionately. Hugo held out his hand for the keys. He swung them on one finger. 'Well, what shall we do? Had you better stay the night in my flat?' He sounded less than pressing.

'Thank you for the kind offer, but little Percy will be waiting patiently at Phlox for me. I'll have to get home. How mortifying! Causing trouble after you've given me such a jolly evening. Would you be able to take me in your car?'

'Then yours will be stranded here.'

'Well, I don't know. Perhaps I ought to take a taxi home?'

'Your car would still be here.' Hugo unlocked the Morris.

'Oh dear. What a duffer I am. You are good to me.'

They both climbed in, he behind the wheel. 'There's nothing for it but for me to take you to Fulking. What's the form with buses to Brighton?'

'Absolutely no problem,' Roweena assured him, massaging her

temples with closed eyes. 'They run at every hour. But I couldn't think of you fagging over on the bus. You have my guarantee. I will drive you back after breakfast tomorrow.' She wondered how much bread there was in the house.

They travelled mostly in silence. Hugo wondered where he'd be put to spend the night. Would there be a bed made up in the spare room? Perhaps Roweena would save herself bother and stick him into Octavia's bed. He drove the silent dark miles of countryside, seeing himself ensconced there with an abandoned nightie – or possibly a long-length T shirt – screwed up in his hand.

The hall at Phlox Cottage, dim and musty-smelling, welcomed him with its familiarity. There was the grandfather clock, the Jacobean-style chairs and the stained oak chest. Roweena led him straight upstairs, calling dotingly to Percy who confronted them on the landing, quivering with nerves. Roweena scooped him under her arm and with comforting questions and answers, vanished into her own bedroom. Hugo wondered if the dachshund slept there with her.

He hung about uneasily until Roweena drifted out again, Percy at her heels, and he found himself billeted in the spare bedroom. The bed was ready made, but with no attention to detail; and there was an odd scrap of blanket lying on top. The towel she remembered to hand him emanated a stale doggy odour. When alone, sniffing the square of blanket, Hugo's fears were realised. He bent over the pillow, suspiciously examining it for clues. No hairs. No stains. Looked fresh enough. But that tell-tale smell . . . He wondered if Isabel and Oliver were as squeamish when their turns came.

He went slowly downstairs to the hall, and checked his watch with the grandfather clock. He could hear Roweena's creaking tread on the floor above. He felt a great peace steal over him, listening to those homely movements and the clock's fruity ticking, and following the rhythmic pendulum through its glass panel. There was dignity and peace everywhere in the world one might suppose, standing in that hall . . .

Hugo sat on the oak chest. He listened for the clock's occasional hiccup. It was hard, even now, to believe he was there not long

133

before midnight, the companion and protector to the Recluse. What a turn-up for the books!

He heard a cistern flush, then unhurried feet descending the stairs. At the bottom she started violently. 'Good heavens – what a shock!'

'I'm sorry.' Hugo stood.

'No, sit down. It's a lovely private place to gather one's wits. You'll never guess why you startled me.'

'You took me for a ghost?'

'I believe I did – very nearly. Lily says she once saw a robed monk standing under that clock. But I tend to ignore the things she tells me.'

'I hope I don't look too much like a monk,' Hugo said drily. 'I was wondering – may I use the telephone, Roweena?'

'Go ahead. The Cottage is at your disposal as long as you stay.'

She left him to his phoning, going down the passage into the kitchen, murmuring under her breath.

Hugo dialed a London number. 'James? Yes, it's me . . .' He spoke softly. Roweena might be listening. 'I'm sorry I haven't shown up. . . . In Fulking. Yes, Fulking, the Ransome place . . . Not till the weekend. I've got a temporary change of routine, you see . . . Schedule in reverse . . . Well, call it evasive action if you like . . . No, perfectly all right, just a slight cold . . . Hell, I don't know . . . See you late-ish on Friday I hope. No, wait. Make that mid-morning Saturday – if that's all right.' He hung up with a frown. He must remember to give James the notion of himself as a disembodied monk.

Roweena was approaching, bringing with her a strong aromatic scent. 'I've just spilt my trusty oil of lavender. Such a waste. It stops one from being eaten alive in the garden. Slopped it over a newspaper review that Nicholas wanted kept, will you believe it? D'you like a nightcap, by the way?'

'Such as?'

'Oh, just a nursery drink. Percy likes it, and I shall have some.'

'I'll be with you in five minutes. May I think about it?'

'What a bore I am! You haven't finished your phoning. You'll have forgotten what you wanted to say.'

Hugo waited. He held his breath. He saw Roweena blossoming before his eyes, transforming into a younger creature with voluptuous arms, who sucked him against pillowy breasts, ultimately to destroy him. He might never get away!

He dialed Buckland Crescent. A short wait. Hugo resumed his perch on the chest and traced its crude carving with a finger. 'Octavia? How are you, Angel?' He planted his elbows on his knees. 'Yes, it is a bit late. Sorry about that. Now, what have you to report after two days without me? . . . Good, good . . . Yes, it went really well . . . Oh, we had dinner, and talked about you . . . No, in the end I didn't tell her. I'm a coward, and – you know – after our quarrel . . . Darling, I'm sure that all will be fine – as sure as I can possibly can be. That's why I had to phone.'

The sound of her voice fired him. 'Darling Octavia,' he said, leaning against the wall with emotions of his own. 'You never give up. That's what I first loved about you . . . As a matter of fact, I'm at Phlox Cottage. I'm staying the night.'

Whatever the music behind her, it was horribly insistent. He wanted to say, Turn that off! She was expostulating at his being with her mother, half indignant, half amused. He countered with, 'Is that Nick I hear in the background? Oliver then? . . . Oh, I don't think I know Julian. Haven't heard of him.' So he needn't exist, his tone implied. 'Never mind that, or why I'm about to sneak into your childhood bed. Tell me one thing: Where does master Percy sleep in this house? . . . That's a relief. But when he's on his own, where then? . . . Oh dear . . . Well listen darling, I just had to tell you again how bloody awful I felt over our row at the Albany. It was completely my fault. I've been rather tense since my trip. But that's no excuse . . . Well now, I thought I'd stay at the flat for the rest of the week, give myself some sea air . . .'

Someone had interrupted her. The music had ceased. Hugo felt exposed at both ends of the line. 'Darling, are you there? Look, if you'll let me, I want to give you a special dinner at the weekend. We'll go to English's . . . Right. That's wonderful. Now, if you're coming on your usual train we'll meet at Brighton station . . . Darling, don't worry about Max Fortune. Just leave at the usual time. . . . Don't worry about me, I feel fitter every day . . . Promise? . . . Yes . . . Now listen, all will be well when we meet, and I long for that moment.'

A milk drink awaited him in the kitchen. Roweena was sitting at the table, also waiting, and Percy waited at her ankles. The dog yapped shrilly and ran in a circle. Hugo eyed the malted beverage, and Percy's milky chin. Then he contemplated Roweena. The image she presented was so unselfconsciously batty, so serene, that he bent over her as a husband. The cloche hat was still on her head, quite forgotten. Like a husband, he removed it, and kissed her deliberately on the temple. Then he repeated the kiss very gently on the other side, ignoring Percy's rage.

Roweena looked up at him, searching for something appropriate to say. He smiled with a comfortable simplicity, and sat beside her. Lifting his milk, he said humourously, 'Here's to us both.'

Chapter 34

'How is the dear old Rapier?' Octavia slid inside. 'It seems so long since I went anywhere in it.'

They glided down Queen's Road towards the Clock Tower through a cold fog drifting up from the sea. Hugo explained how his work had advanced and she filled him in on the continuing saga of life at API.

'But before we talk about us, may I ask you something?' Octavia rested a hand on his thigh and watched him changing gear. 'About my mother, actually. You like her, don't you?'

'Yes. I can honestly say I'm fond of her.'

'Do you really enjoy her company?'

The fog parted to each side of them and streamed past in ghostly ranks. He touched her hand, then returned his to the wheel.

'Do you?' she repeated.

'I do, as a matter of fact.'

They continued in a silence which was broken only by the windscreen wipers. Hugo slowed. The fog thickened, piling like ethereal snowdrifts over their bonnet. A situation which should have drawn them together began already to isolate them, to obscure their meanings from each other.

'Yes,' Hugo resumed with cavalier insouciance, as though after careful consideration. 'I've a great admiration for Roweena. When I hear her describe her wartime experiences and that difficult period after the war I appreciate her courage. She doesn't let one see the knocks she's taken.'

Staring at a fog-bound window, Octavia affected indifference. The admirable Roweena whom he described presumably still hadn't a clue he was poised to become a member of her family. 'Little does she guess you're shaping up as son-in-law.'

Hugo permitted himself a smile. 'Your mother, as well as being the paragon I paint, is extremely perceptive. I'll tell you more at dinner.'

After touring East Street and the sea front, they discovered a parking space outside the Brighton Town Hall. They walked through covered arcades to Regency Square, down a narrow passage and so to English's.

There was a tank of trout outside the restaurant. Voices from the bar downstairs wafted into the dank sea mist. Rank fishy odours seeped up from the sea front. Hugo took Octavia's elbow and, guided into this extrovert atmosphere, her spirits lifted. She started to mount the stairs, Hugo close behind her.

They had an excellent table, against the wall, and sat together on the banquette so that both could enjoy the room.

'I ask myself if you've grown any less callow since I last brought you here,' he whispered, bending his head towards hers. He smoothed out his napkin. 'I'm sorry I was so patronizing in the Albany, darling.'

She met his kindly eyes. 'It seems a long time ago, coming here with you and Muth. And James. I prefer not to think of that occasion at the Albany. It spoils the happy times there.' She reflected a minute. 'I believe we've both changed a lot.'

'For better, or worse?'

'Irrelevant. We aren't married yet.' She let the remark sink in; then added, 'Perhaps I'm not so callow. But there's one sin I should confess.' He looked expectant. 'That Barry mansion. I did nothing about it. Forgot.'

'Yes. I fear you're a flighty creature.' He shook his head and picked up the menu. 'Your concentration is easily seduced.'

They made their order and raised their glasses to each other. Then Hugo said without warning, 'Do you ever have any doubts about us?'

She switched her blue gaze on him. 'How can you ask such a thing?' Exquisite eyes, he thought, like aquamarine.

She was saying to herself, this trip to Laos has compromised his integrity. Spoiled his dream. Spoiled his feelings for me. He has changed – but it's not his fault.

'I wondered,' he said.

'But . . .' Octavia groped for words. 'Why ask me now? Don't spoil our dinner.'

''I'm sorry. I'd looked to the future for a moment.'

Smiling, she lay back on the plush seat. 'Hurrah! Never too late.'

From the heart of the restaurant pumped the lilt of a tango. Memories of the fifties, lyrical and shallow, peppered with sensations of Vivian. Hugo remained serious. 'You don't actually know me very well,' he pursued, his voice low. She became infected by his solemnity, poking at the tablecloth with bent head. 'If ever you were to have doubts about me darling girl, it must be now. Before it really is too late.'

'How am I supposed to know you better? By waiting another six months? I'm only ignorant about what you conceal from me.'

He compressed his lips, half amused, feeling his way towards an explanation. 'We've never had a serious talk of this sort before. I'm sorry if I've depressed you, bringing up doubts. It's horrid of me. But I've had it on my conscience.' He lifted her hand and brought it under the drooping cloth, with his own. She felt his pulse against her palm – perhaps it was her pulse. Their two hands lay together, containing that mute throb like a frantic animal they were protecting.

'What have you had on your conscience?' she asked heavily.

'Your happiness.' He squeezed her fingers. 'Not only now, but always. You so lightly made it my responsibility. I want you to reconsider. To look at me afresh.'

'I thought I'd shown my love for you; and my trust in you.'

'But you've loved with such recklessness! You make me doubt myself. That's the truth.' Pleasures of their friendship lit his mind, while he tried to ignore them.

'Is that all? So what more can I do to prove you're the best man on earth? That I'm the one to have self-doubts?'

Having uttered her rhetorical question, she fell prey to just those doubts about herself. Was that what he was hinting at?

Hugo drew a deep breath. 'For example, what would you say if I told you I'd been seeing Diana this week? Sleeping with her, even?'

'I'd say you couldn't love me. Of course.' She spoke calmly.

'Well, I do love you. But I've been thinking of seeing Diana. And I can't explain why.'

Simple acceptance was beyond her. She was at the mercy

of jealousy in its first, most acute form. He was putting her to an obscure test. What in the world could she say? Isabel's denunciations of older men came back to her.

'However,' Hugo observed, 'however we look at our relationship, I'm the one to gain, you are the one who stands to lose. When we have children Octavia, you'll grow up with them. I'll find myself getting slow. And you'll never catch me up. You wouldn't want to. But as our children grow older, they and you will find me a disappointment and a bore. We may grow apart. You'll tire of me.'

'That's so banal,' she cried impatiently. 'It can apply to any couple, give or take some bad luck. Or accidents. Do you imagine I haven't thought of it all a hundred times? I may seem impetuous. But you also know how introspective I can be. I internalize a lot, and I've thought about us through every contingency. I suppose,' she added more humbly, 'this is why you avoid the issue with my mother.' She glanced up again. 'If you think I'm too idealistic to forgive you for wanting an older woman – this Diana – you're wrong.'

They sat back while a small plate of cod roes and an elaborate prawn cocktail were put before them. Then Hugo said, 'Your defiance, which used to be my chief concern, now seems to be my chief asset.'

She clung to him as discreetly as she could, responding to the humour in his voice. She began to laugh nervously, laying her head against his forearm on the cloth. He sat as though thunderstruck while she felt nothing but rapture. Raising her head, she began delving into her prawn cocktail. Hugo lifted a fork and prodded the supine roes. He could hardly get the mess down his throat.

'Eat up,' she coaxed, sensitive to his mood again. The look in her eyes almost brought tears to his. 'Dear Octavia,' he said. He fumbled for her hand and this time he crushed it into his lap with a force that made her wince and stare at him, cheeks glowing. He refused to meet her eyes. 'Look,' he said, 'try to understand what I'm telling you. Try to understand.' But he couldn't go on. Her face was bleak with the dread of hearing he had no love for her.

'I'm trying to warn you,' he said, his breath louder than his words in their secluded corner, 'that I can't trust or understand myself. That I'll disappoint you. Don't throw yourself away on a man you hardly know. Remember what happened to my first marriage.'

Chapter 35

Their waiter was hovering like a bird of prey. Hugo nodded to confirm all was well. Octavia's fingers were against his wrist. 'Don't doubt that I love you. There may be a dozen reasons to make me hesitate – but not that. Listen, I'll tell you a few things . . .'

Octavia listened.

'In Vientiane for example,' he started to explain, 'one day I went to the British Embassy. There I found a letter from you in my pigeon-hole. A Vietnamese girl sat behind the Reception counter, a willowy creature with French manners. When I'd spoken to the Information Officer, I asked this girl where she'd bought her sinh – the long silk skirt, you know. Then the Ambassador came though from the Chancery and I went outside with him. We chatted on the steps while his chauffeur brought the Humber round. I went back into the Embassy and the girl told me she'd got her skirt from the Morning Market.

'I went off in a taxi and got out on a space opposite the Market. What a road! Fruit skins and mangy dogs strewn everywhere, and ruts about six inches deep. This was the great centre of a city mark you, into which divers funds, faiths and bloods have been poured. French aspirations blended with Eastern fatalism, comedy with tragedy. The road I crossed was crowned with a replica of the Arc de Triomphe. But the Vientiane monument was already enjoying the decline of an antiquity.' Hugo signaled to the wine waiter. Determined to unburden himself, to what end he wasn't clear, he needed even more encouragement than Octavia's silence.

'I picked my way around squatting women,' he resumed, and then the wine arrived with tactless panache, followed by sole and lobster. Octavia began to eat like a prisoner whose death sentence might yet be commuted.

'There was a rancid stench of rotten fish in the air – just to whet your appetite still more. Also pungent oils and raw meat.

Some of the old hags grinned at me with their shriveled faces while they sat on their hunkers, chewing betel.'

Hugo also made a show of eating. Octavia noticed that his hand shook as he held his knife. He swallowed two mouthfuls, then plunged back into his narrative, and Octavia wondered if it was his love for Laos or a fear of exposure that made him so diffuse.

'I'd come to a complex of fragile shops. There were cotton shirts and cheap belts and household necessities, all hanging up by my ears and sprawling around me. The intersecting passages were narrow and everything chaotic. I pushed my way to a skirt depot. There were somber greens, browns, maroons of shot silk. Some were heavily bordered with gold thread. Which colour for Octavia?' Hugo moved his lobster from one side of his plate to the other and drank more wine.

'What about your liver?' Octavia demanded, involuntarily breaking the spell. 'Lobster thermidor and cods roes – and wine. You'll be ill again.'

'I'll stint myself tomorrow,' he said with an ironic smile. 'I was telling you about the skirts. A richly bordered sinh would cost one thousand five hundred kips. I was quite willing to pay that, but I couldn't decide which. I kept holding them up and the woman called someone over, and this young person let herself be decked out in one sinh after another to help me choose. Then I settled for – well, one of them. I've got it for you – but there hasn't been the right moment to give it yet.'

She tried to smile, and pressed his hand.

'I left the Market and drove to my hotel amidst the usual conglomeration of Mercedes and buffalo wagons and samlaw carriages. The bar was supported by Reuters, Newsweek, other pressmen. Time Magazine had sent in their top man from Saigon. Bad sign. I took refuge in a corner. I was hungry for news of you. I was already imagining you wearing the sinh I'd bought, and it occurred to me that you'd need a solid gold belt – the sort they smuggle in from Burma I believe. I planned to get one. Then I tore open your letter – very carefully, because I preserved the envelopes as well.'

Hugo swallowed another mouthful. He remarked to Octavia, as to a person now rather than an audience, 'Don't eat it if you don't want to.' But Octavia stoutly persevered.

Hugo went on, 'I read all through your spirited activities. But instead of enjoying them, I felt my spirits ebb. My vitality couldn't compete with yours. I was stung by your allusions to other people, other friends. I realize now it was a bout of hepatitis.'

Octavia finally gave up eating, suddenly close to laughter. Hugo continued to confide, like someone in a trance.

'There was a French colonial mansion opposite the hotel, the official residence of the Minister of the Interior. It was shuttered up and surrounded by green vegetation. Another of Souvanna Phouma's ministers had been murdered in it only the previous week. England seemed remote as I looked at that house. You too were so remote. That letter should have made me hit the ceiling for joy. But it filled me with distance and years separating us. And the endless civil conflict in Laos. Take your mind back to our first dinner here. James got steamed up about Suez. About the invasion of Hungary. But the civil war in Laos has been going on for twenty years – and nobody gives a damn.'

Octavia broke in, 'Hugo . . .' She was recalling the charming way he'd first talked about Laos at Phlox Cottage. Now he was proselytizing like the Ancient Mariner. 'Hugo . . .'

He parried her with a firm gesture. 'I fretted about you all that night. I pictured you dancing in London with young Oliver and young Julian. How could I be sure my passion wasn't the emotion of an aging egotist?' He wiped his forehead impatiently. 'You see, Octavia, this is what I'm trying to say . . . and I was down with a bug from the Mekong in good earnest, and my life became one bloody hell.'

Hugo checked himself. He began pushing at the table to free his legs. 'I'm sorry, I really don't feel very well now. I can't face any more food. Could you forgive me if we leave?'

She hadn't said another word, but he hailed their waiter, paid the bill and stumbled outside. Octavia ran to catch him up and grasped his arm, prepared for him to shake her off. His weakness, whether psychological or physical, put her own distress to flight.

They walked to the Rapier. When they were sitting inside, he turned and kissed her mouth. 'Don't be upset, dearest girl. I'll take you home, then get on my way. I'll spend the weekend in London.'

'But why?' Her voice was so low he hardly heard her. 'You

144

could stay at the Cottage again. Muth and I can look after you.' She remembered as she spoke that the spare room was needed for Isabel.

He started the engine with authority. She made herself elaborately comfortable. He revved the accelerator, let the car slide backwards and pulled brusquely away. He said, 'We'll be better for another day or so apart. I've still got the remnants of that cold. Your family don't want it.'

Octavia ran her tongue over the germs that were supposedly on her lips, hating his prevarications. He concentrated on the dark road, seeming matter-of-fact again, weaving a route by devious back streets. Defiant and obstinate she may once have been, but the shock he'd given her had surely killed her spirit. She doubted if she'd live until morning.

'Don't be sad,' he said. They sped to the top of Dyke Road then launched themselves over the Downs like fugitives of the night.

'Don't leave me in this mood. I can't understand you ....'

'Of course not. I'll never forgive myself for hoping you could. I've ruined our dinner and made you very unhappy.'

'You mean you had to be cruel?' She glanced at him.

Touché. The thought gave him a jolt. He drove on in silence, shut away from her. She added, 'Never say any of it again. If you need to have Diana, give me up. Otherwise, give her up. Never talk about it.'

'I won't. I'll try to have faith in myself as well as in you.'

His words numbed her into a withdrawal that lasted until they drove up to the house. There, she lay against him for so long, her head on his shoulder, that he supposed she'd fallen asleep.

Chapter 36

'I wish this letter to be dispatched by special messenger Miss Ransome. Kindly ensure that a copy is placed on file under Recreation.' Isabel spoke in Max Fortune's stagey accent. 'Pay attention please.'

Octavia turned away from her bedroom window. She made an effort to appear composed and attentive. Isabel, without much inside information, was trying to cheer her friend's languishing spirits.

Isabel shook the paper in her hand. 'This is what I've written: 'Dear Sir, It is with increasing dismay that I witness the treatment meted out by drakes to ducks during the mating season in all our London parks equipped with water fowl. It is scarcely reasonable to suggest that the better nature of the drake be appealed to. But surely anyone with a modest sense of fair play and decency must revolt at the sight of these savaged, exhausted, frequently half-drowned victims of masculine aggression – which I shall not forebear to add, is all too apparent in every strata of life. I would strenuously urge the keepers of these birds to segregate the sexes in the spring, and force a system of controlled mating for breeding purposes only. If any accidental frustration or loss of ego is sustained by the males, let me say that it might serve as a salutary example to this sex in general. I am Sir, Yours etc." Isabel paused. "Nicholas Ransome."

Octavia smiled. 'That's a bit brutal, isn't it?'

Pastoral outings with Hugo. Strolling in St James's Park eating Danish pastries and tossing pieces to the ducks. And drakes. Everything happy and everything just.

'Drakes are brutal. Nick's been brutal in his gentle way. He doesn't realize it though. That's his trouble.'

'That's your trouble, you mean. He lacks the cave man instinct. You want more action from him.'

'I don't want my neck chewed! Or my head shoved under

water. But I wish he'd touch me somewhere – sometimes. He was so sweet during Fortune's hellish progress into chauvinism. It made all the difference.' Unlike Oliver, Isabel added to herself. Tavia had always seemed to hanker after Olly until Hugo became serious. Perhaps mature men had the edge after all.

'Nick's nicer for not being conceited and over-sexed. I can almost imagine him writing a letter like that. I'm ninety-five per cent sure he's in love with you.'

Isabel stood up, stretching restlessly. Talk about sex always made her feel she had energy to burn. 'Never mind 'in love.' Just love would be nice from Nicky. I want your faultless brother to look the word up. I'm going for a walk. Tell him to come with me.' She moved towards the door. 'Where shall we walk? Wakey wakey Miss Ransome! I'll have to write a letter from YOU to the Times. Remind me to buy a daily copy by the way, or we might miss Nick's.'

There came a shout from downstairs. 'Where are you?' Footsteps approached the landing. 'Hello! What's going on?' Nicholas came in, carrying his blazer and circulating his shoulders like an athlete limbering up. 'You do realise it's only twenty minutes before church?'

'Are we going to church? Who's We?'

'Oh, come on Tavia. We've always gone when Muth is motivated to go. It's nice to show a bit of solidarity. Anyway, I like going for reasons of my own.'

Isabel caught Octavia's eye. She took hold of him and steered him to the bed. 'Lie down.'

He complied, stretching out on his stomach with a piece of paper in his hand. 'What's the idea?'

Isabel knelt over his back and began to massage his shoulders. He groaned and winced, raising his head in protest and staring at Isabel's letter. 'Who's been writing to the newspaper?'

'Hey!' Isabel grabbed it away. 'Lie still. If I can cure my tennis shoulder, I can probably cure yours. But only if you collaborate.'

'You must be more gentle.'

Isabel whacked behind her, like a rider striking a horse. Watching them made Octavia think what a wonderful thing, to be uninhibited; to be confident that love lay just ahead ...

Nicholas was laughing into the pillow. Isabel was saying, 'If the church bells weren't calling us to higher matters I'd have your shirt off and some deep heat rubbed into your bottom.'

'Oh you wouldn't, you wouldn't!' cried Nicholas in mock distress. 'Not my bottom!'

'Whose bottom?' Roweena asked, appearing in the open doorway. 'You're not suffering from piles at your age I hope, Nicholas? Think of all the sedentary years still to come.' She walked into the room and looked more closely at the young people crowded on Octavia's bed.

Isabel removed herself and pulled the quilt straight. 'Just giving his shoulder a rub, Mrs Ransome. He says he's strained it. Funny how he only has tennis shoulder when he's afraid he won't win.'

Percy trotted into the room and joined Nicholas on the bed. 'Does that pillow smell of dog?' Roweena asked. 'I'll tell you why. It was a remark Hugo made when he stayed overnight. He more or less informed me that the spare bed smelt of Percy. Well, I daresay it did. Percy always liked the peace and quiet of the spare room.'

'It doesn't smell of dog in the least,' said Octavia. 'Get him OFF please Nicky.' Nicholas and Percy left the bed together. 'Wasn't it rather offensive, having your guest complain like that?'

'It was a bit.' Roweena spoke with no trace of rancor or of shame. 'Percy doesn't like Hugo. That's all there is to it. But you'd think a man who's used to roughing it wouldn't object to the smell of dog. Nobody's asked me about that evening, have they? No one has asked how sharing the bathroom worked out – and what Hugo and I talked about!'

'How did the bathroom work out?' Nicholas asked. 'I hope it was richly comic.' He was aware of the way Isabel was watching him adjust his blazer.

'Aren't you interested, Octavia?' her mother demanded, feeling let down by her children's indifference.

'No. Not specially.'

'Well, you may be surprised to learn that he persuaded the old cabbage to feel young and frivolous again. He wined me and dined me and was a perfect gentleman, fagging right out into the country afterwards as though it was his greatest pleasure.'

Octavia stared at her. 'Describe dinner then.'

'We went to a Chinese restaurant. The Heavenly something.

There's no need to look so disapproving. Come on, we really must be off.' Roweena moved purposefully towards the door, talking as she went. 'Anyone would think it was sinful for two middle-aged people to share a companiable night.'

'Hugo's quite a sly boots,' said Nicholas. 'He doesn't just function on one level. I rather admire that.'

His mother said, 'Hugo isn't sly. He's reticent, like me. He's reserved. Isn't that what you mean?'

'No,' answered Nicholas. He was overcome by how lovely Isabel was. All that weekend, the thoughts kept coming. Such dark eyes. So slender. And yet, a moment ago, how solid on the base of his spine. A really womanly weight. She seemed fonder of him than of Oliver, no question. She never threatened to tear the shirt off Oliver's back or rub deep heat into HIS bottom. What a bind Muth was, bringing up piles! Supposedly a son's best friend. Who needed enemies with a mother around! He longed to take Isabel on a walk and make violent love to her. But self-control, that was the watchword. He and Olly had read a book about it at school. Dr Eustace Chesser; how girls needed more time than boys, and therefore boys must exercise self control.

'We mustn't be late for the service. Shall I lock the back door and leave Percy in the kitchen, Mrs Ransome?' he heard Isabel asking. She got a kick out of going to their ancient country church. She'd said it to him in private, and he believed her.

'You all go. I can't come,' Octavia said.

'You must,' said Isabel, returning to remonstrate while there was still time.

'I can't be sick in church. I'm feeling very sick.'

Her friend shot her a glance of great significance. Receiving and understanding it caused Octavia a genuine nausea that made her fold over. Good heavens, had Isabel ever been more hopelessly wrong? She promised to lie down, to be kind to Percy, to be recovered in time for an afternoon walk. She couldn't wait for them to leave, to hear them driving away to Poynings. It was like a wheel coming full circle. History repeating itself. She dashed a rapid note and propped it against the hump-backed clock for one of them to find.

Ten minutes later, she checked her purse for money, dragged on a jacket and walked out of the house.

Chapter 37

She emerged from the Underground in Lower Regent Street. A thin chain of traffic around Eros, modest crowds circulating with no apparent purpose past closed shops. Octavia hovered outside Swan and Edgars, aware that once she might have been drawn to its windows, tantalized by goods it was fun to want. Now they filled her with contempt for the human race.

Driven like an autumn leaf along the pavement, she meandered in the direction of the Albany. It drew her like a magnet, despite a constant reluctance to take that initiative. She began hurrying, to meet the challenge and get it over. Swerving in to the courtyard, she leaped the front steps. A porter with whom she had struck up a comradely relationship, greeted her. She hastened past him and he watched her dashing down the inner court.

She kept the momentum going up James's stairway, assuring Hugo that she loved him, telling him that they could get married any time, and in any manner. She wanted to overwhelm him with love, stifle his fears, settle for the nearest registry office. The thudding of her heart was due as much to mental turmoil as to the rush up stairs.

She reached the landing, paused outside the door, uncertain how to announce herself. Was Hugo there? It might be James. Hugo was quite likely to be on the other side of London, deep in a library book.

She laid a hand on the door-knob. Locked. She was turning away even as the door yielded and let her through. The hallway was empty. It received her with chill bachelor disapproval for the first time. How blithely had she felt welcomed before!

As though silence were germane to her success, she tiptoed towards the drawing room. There she stopped again, shivering with self-induced suspense. Would Hugo be annoyed to see her? Past experience had shown that his habits and his moods altered with illness.

But he only had a cold! Unless that lobster had got to his liver...

Octavia opened the drawing room door and made a bold appearance. The room was empty. That was disconcerting. This had to be the limit. She'd have to creep out and find somewhere else to go in London. She moved softly towards the bedroom and pushed the door wide.

Two people were standing near the bed. One was Hugo. The other was also a man. He had his back towards her. He was naked.

Hugo was wearing a sarong, the one he had bought himself at the Morning Market. They were posed with their arms about each other. Hugo's hand was on James's thigh. Octavia stood like an enchanted interloper, filled with astonishment, then dawning comprehension.

James Wedge revolved in a gliding movement. How pale he was, and almost hairless. A translucent fish in the lustrous lamp-lit chamber. Like protagonists in a stylized dance sequence, their pose lapsed.

Octavia backed into the open door, but Hugo flung out his hand to stay her. 'Octavia.'

She stopped, open even now to the persuasion that what she'd seen was a hoax. Hugo had only to utter some commonplace, James to sink into a chair, with his complex smile.

But James stood revealed before her, epicurean features disdainful. Fascinated, she kept her eyes on him, unable to look at Hugo. She wished she could rationalize what appeared to be such extravagance.

Hugo pushed James aside and came reassuringly across, quite unconcerned. He offered her his kindest smile. Then James closed up behind him. He touched Hugo's waist and suddenly the large-checked sarong twitched to the carpet. Hugo floundered for it and Octavia retreated again.

'There dear,' she heard James murmur.

She descended the steps in pairs, sped through the Albany precincts and into Vigo Street at the back. Even with the Albany behind her she continued the same rapid pace, to escape the state of her mind.

There were interminable delays getting to Swiss Cottage. Once she had arrived, the situation improved. Thinking could be hindered by focusing on familiar scenes. She reached the Buckland Crescent flat, mounted the stairs and threw herself on the bed.

Her experience receded as she lay there. She recovered her poise with the certainty of reason after bad dreams. She rolled carefully on to her back, afraid to upset the equilibrium. Behind closed eyes she saw Hugo coming towards her in his black and red check sarong, with his very dear smile, proffering the hand of goodness and love.

Chapter 38

In the Albany, Hugo was in reality gesturing with his hands in James's direction.

'Well Hugo, you are quite the young Rakehell,' James was saying ironically, more in sorrow than in anger.

'A reputation must, I suppose, always follow the career? It's clear my career has finished.'

'Even a Rakehell's career has to finish some time.' James spoke gently, massaging lemon-scented lanolin into his fingers and wrists, while sprawled on the four poster bed. By now he was wearing slacks and a smoking jacket, one of Liberty's Chinese silks, dragon-studded, swags of gold against as a rich bottle green. His dark hair gleamed with the special pomade obtained from a barber in St James's. He added, 'His checkered career, that is, if I read this particular young Rakehell aright. Give up the pretense, it's the only way out. Sever all ties with those people. At once.'

Thoroughly confused, Hugo could only temporize. Discussion of the matter, and apologies for it, seemed equally intolerable. He said, with an attempt at buoyancy, 'My inclination not to give the girl up is so strong I think it will overpower me.'

'You have a weak character, Hugo.' James smiled with the mitigating fondness of a parent. 'Telephone the mother. You owe her a word of warning on imminent filial hysteria. Telephone her this instant.'

'And explain that life is paradoxical. I'm an ogre, and she and her daughter importunate dupes.'

'Exactly.'

Hugo poured some whisky from a decanter which James had carelessly left on his chest-of-drawers. He carried it out of the bedroom and sat on the couch under James's bookshelves. Aware that James had strayed in his wake, he selected a volume of Restoration comedy and began to idle from play to play, reading wherever his eye was caught.

'Come along, come along,' James briskly urged, strolling the carpet as though modeling his smoking jacket before an audience. 'Pull yourself together. Doubtless there's a Laotian proverb which sums the situation up or, if not, you can invent one. Your last offering might do: When the elephants fight, the grass gets trampled. You'll hear the phone drop to the floor, and the lady with it.'

Hugo didn't trouble to look up. 'That's a perfectly authentic Laotian proverb. But you've remembered it wrong. Buffaloes, not elephants. As for the lady, you speak from ignorance. She'd brush me aside with an account of Toblat's latest adventures in wonderland. My confession wouldn't be noticed.'

'Toblat? Can that be her dog?'

'No no. Her spirit. I refer to an alphabetical jest over my name that was made during . . . Planchette.' Some ruthless influence impelled him to meet James's eyes. 'I don't suppose all novices at the game are given such preferential treatment.'

James's brandished his cigar. 'My dear man! You should be truly grateful to me for releasing you from such perils. I shudder to think how those females might have perverted your good nature: your name being translated into a kind of bastard Chinese, your soul manipulated by disembodied pranksters. It's intolerable.'

'Good of you to feel concerned.'

'My only regret over the Ransomes is . . . Nicholas – wasn't it? I dream about that boy.'

'Nicholas happens to be heterosexual. Nothing in it for you, by any stretch of the imagination.'

'A long term, fruitless relationship. Just what I enjoy. I'm a masochist Hugo, you must know that by now.'

'No James. I'm the masochist.' Hugo held his book aloft. 'Do you know, I think I value Vanburgh more than Congreve? He was imprisoned in the Bastille for four years. By mistake. For your information, they thought he was a spy.' Hugo turned the pages. 'Oh Lord Foppington! Would I had your charm.'

James fixed a critical gaze on him again. Hugo glanced up. 'Oh very well, don't nag. I'll phone Roweena in due course.'

The telephone rang. James said, 'That will be for you.'

'You live here, don't forget,' said Hugo, returning to his book.

154

Chapter 39

The important thing was to be out and about.

Octavia was shocked to see Hugo walking towards her along the Embankment. She hurried to meet him. But of course, it wasn't Hugo. She shook with disappointment and relief, her forehead cold and peppery. The incident gave rise to a memory of the mouse he'd given her at the Tate, one of many memories from the days when she and Hugo had played at being in love. She thought, All right – may I never again endure his posturing.

She went into St Martin-in-the-Fields. Sitting in a back row, the skin on her face as tight as if dabbed with ether, she imagined Hugo taking the seat next to hers. Though she dreaded being deceived again, she longed to reconstruct her trust. Hugo had been married. He also loved a woman called Diana. Then – why?

Watching the preacher in his pulpit, an emaciated, stooping figure, she wondered at how God must scorn women. What disadvantages had been heaped on them – physically, emotionally. Staring at the sombre-eyed supplicants around her, spiritual refugees with whom it was humbling to identify, she felt that with so much suffering in the world, misery was hardly misery when inflicted on the loved by the loved.

Back in Swiss Cottage, she passed a coffee bar. Hesitating on the pavement outside, someone brushed insolently past. He glanced over his shoulder, she smiled, and he promptly asked if she was going in. Would she have something with him?

He sat her down at a table by the window and ordered food. Hot air gushed at them from a fan heater. When he was hunched beside her, there began a ritual of questions and answers which revealed the man's poor English. He treated her as if he knew she was unhappy, making soothing gestures with his hands. He laid one of them on Octavia's, a ruse to make her look into his eyes. He told her his home was in Cyprus, and that he hoped to get work in a hotel. Then he noticed she hadn't started the sausages and chips. He coaxed her, rather as Hugo might have done, and after remonstrating to no avail, set to and ate them himself.

'Come with me,' he invited, when he'd finished. Octavia felt faint with the desire to obliterate every finer feeling, to plunge to the depths where pride had no place. It promised to be astonishingly easy. Life was simple, with emotion wiped out. When she'd offered to pay and left the bar, her companion stepped springingly at her side.

He guided her to a red brick building on a corner, from which other foreigners came jumping into the street. He put an arm about her in a loose embrace, displaying her to his neighbours. She was seized with fear. She couldn't follow him into that anonymous block. When her companion urged her forward with his arm, she shook her head at him. He released her and shrugged, and they regarded each other unemotionally. She hastened down the street and round the corner, having failed to do what others did.

Somewhere through the energetic London dusk came a church clock chiming. It was half past seven.

It seemed imperative to keep moving. Buckland Crescent was too intrusive. Nicky would be there by now, probably looking for her. The note she'd left at Phlox Cottage hadn't signaled any alarm, but they'd all be puzzled. Where could she go? She hurried to the Underground and hopped into the first train to arrive.

There was someone beside her. He didn't look at her. She sat in her corner, insulated by noise and the crush of humanity all round. Frantic speeds, hectic stops.

She was walking up from a railway bridge towards the Strand, strangers passing on all sides. There was a man behind her, not quite keeping pace.

She sat over tepid coffee in a raucous bar. The man sat very close. He watched her from time to time. Other men and girls shouted to each other or put their heads together in promiscuous privacy. One of two individuals sat isolated. No-one came to disturb her. She wandered through a park, aware of her loneliness now, as though numbness was wearing off. What was she doing here, alone? She hadn't gone to work. People would be worrying. Shouldn't she go back to Hugo – talk to him, work out a pattern of friendship devised by them both? Surely they owed each other something for the future? She felt calmer than she had since leaving Fulking. Hugo had tried to warn her, but she'd refused to listen. She had forced circumstances her way. If she'd loved Hugo for himself, how different it might have been. He wouldn't have had to humiliate them both by attempted confessions. She had demanded too much – a substitute father and a romantic lover. He had been honest enough to draw the line. He'd helped others, sharing his insights into the mountain tribes he cared about. He'd placed his life in danger. He was heroic, for all his deceptions. Thinking of him in this altruistic vein made her catch her breath.

Traffic was plunging towards Pall Mall, wet tyres hissing at her. She followed the semi-circular sweep of Regent's Street then detoured into Vigo Street where she paused at Hawke's window. A shop for the man-about-town, unobtrusively privileged. Hugo could be an advertisement for those paisley cravats. Octavia sauntered on down Vigo Street, turned up Cork Street, glanced at the Waddington Gallery, found herself outside Sotheby's. Then she hurried back down Bond Street into Piccadilly Circus and towards the Albany again. She was sensitive to cabs crawling in predatory cohorts about Eros, their horns sounding playfully. She should go to Victoria Station. Go home. Haunting the Albany was like hovering at the mouth of hell. Muth would be getting worried.

She sat very stiff in a cinema seat, detached from the entanglements of the film. Images still haunted her: Hugo straddled half-in, half-out of the Rapier. She and Hugo hand-in-hand in a wood, or addressing cows, or dancing slow-motion, or ambling through theatre foyers with all the world at their feet. Or in a taxi in a deep embrace. Running down the Duke of York Steps . . .

She jumped – opening her eyes wide with the sensation of missing a step and falling. She sat on a bus, focusing on the dark pavement. She stretched out her foot and found that she and the bus had parted company. But not so she and the taciturn stranger. She felt light-headed. A long time since she'd eaten. There was always the expectation of Hugo's accepting her in the end.

A glance over the shoulder showed that her shadow had relaxed his pace. He was as much as ten yards behind. In that same moment Octavia saw a taxi cruising quietly. With sudden inspiration as to the possibilities of life, and to the folly she was engaged in, she hailed the taxi and scrambled inside. The door clapped shut and she was swept back in the direction of Swiss Cottage.

Peering through tinted glass at the rear, she saw her shadow had pulled up sharp in his tracks. He calmly watched her tactical departure, before plunging hands into pockets and moving off the opposite way.

With a sense of reincarnation, Octavia let her thought speed ahead. This car was in her pay, hired to take her where she commanded. That was the life! She'd go no further than Buckland Crescent today. In the flat, still unanswered, was her formal offer of employment from the Foreign Office. The thing was to leave London, leave England. She was to become a member of H M Diplomatic Service, appropriately joining the Secret Service.

And here she was, out-smarting that pest in the darkness. If Hugo advised her to steer clear of 'the Friends' – well, what did he know about her anyway?

I'll see him before I go, she decided. He still hasn't given me the Laotian sinh he took so long to choose. I'll say a sporting goodbye, listen to more good advice, and let him patronize my decisions. And we'll part the best of friends.

Chapter 40

Earlier that day Roweena had been sitting on a rusty seat in a fetid segment of the garden. It was a moist autumnal evening. She held a sprig of crushed sage, the scent of which rose cloyingly in an ochre atmosphere.

She sat perfectly still, leaf mould covering the toes of her shoes. The grass at her feet had withered. This corner had a peculiar smell, an ambiance all its own. There was the stench of rotten vegetation, and the lachrymose secrecy that evolves from a shadowy place where pets have been buried.

Percy, whose condition she now feared was serious, lay like a mummified child on her lap. His swaddling wraps covered him from muzzle to tail, which was folded neatly inside. Was it instinct that a recuperative spirit lurked there, a place she rarely visited, amongst the little dead bodies? Or a sombre compulsion that had brought her to this spot? With her two-fold anxieties, it fitted her mood exactly. How leaden she felt! How horribly low.

Sage. Emotive herb. An echo of Hugo in the summer house, or telephoning in the dimness of her hall. So strange, to have seen him there, like Gilbert come back to life. Quite at home, as though he'd heard the clock's deep ticks from his boyhood. Dear, kind Hugo at Planchette, when all might have been fiasco without his good humour. That aroma certainly brought him to mind.

His embraces.

Now, since the phone call, an abrupt farewell. His friendship withdrawn. Some muddle, some emotional mistake, academic failure – the ominous Mr Wedge. And Octavia disappointed. The blossom of her own Indian summer nipped in the bud.

And where was Octavia? No trace of her at Buckland Crescent, according to Nicholas, although she'd evidently spent the night there. At least I know why she abandoned poor Percy, Roweena thought, if Hugo had made her unhappy. She would hardly be thinking of Percy, and noticing he was a shivering wreck. No blame attached. But fancy Hugo making her miserable! She was much too young to be affected by him in that way. An immature girl by the standards of the thirties, let alone the sixties.

I believed he was fond of me, Roweena thought without sentimentality. We were like dear beasts together, absurd in our mutual need and affection. She drew the sage leaves slowly through looped finger and thumb, listening to their fragile rustle. Octavia must, surely, have gone back to the flat by now? She would know when Nicholas telephoned.

Her bell was shrilling. She stood up and moved with bent head towards the house.

No-one at the front door. Roweena, perfectly unhurried, went to the back. She recoiled from the door at finding Lily Falange waiting patiently. Lily, on a Monday evening?

'Come in,' she invited. Percy yapped feebly. Lily stepped in. She removed a limp wool hat and set it on the scullery draining-board. 'Why does the wall look so different out there? So bare. What's been taken away?'

'Only some Virginia creeper. I'd grown rather tired of it.'

Lily's eyes twinkled at her. 'You took against it, then?'

'What can I do for you Lily?' Roweena leaned against the scullery door.

Lily clasped her plump hands. 'May I stay a moment, Mrs Ransome?'

As Roweena retreated to the kitchen, Lily shut the connecting door as if barring companions her neighbour couldn't see. 'I thought I'd better call.'

'Yes?' Roweena simulated activity, pushing two jardinières together on the window-ledge and pouring water into them from an angular copper can.

Percy stared out from his blanket with neurotic attention.

'I had my little Gathering this afternoon,' Lily said apologetically. Her voice was as warm and timid as her expression. 'My sister, one or two other folk . . .'

Roweena turned round, and Lily, feeling it appropriate to continue said, 'We were expecting to be in touch with the Doctor. But out of the blue . . .' She paused, re-clasping her hands. 'Out of the blue we were visited by a Stranger.' The hazel eyes wavered.

160

Roweena thought, If I could only ask her to go and clean the bath. Something useful.

Lily laid hold of a chair. 'There was another warning concerning your family. Only I don't want to alarm you, naturally.'

'Really?' Roweena gave a brittle laugh. 'You'd sooner alarm me unnaturally? Tell me more.' You viper, she thought, eyeing the other woman's coils of hair.

'It was garbled, I can say that without disrespect.' Lily gave her shy smile. 'May I sit down? My hip's paining me today.' Seated with legs placed squarely, blue woolen bloomers were displayed to the knees.

'You say you had a warning from a stranger,' Roweena repeated. 'Probably it was a mistake. You know I'm not the least psychic.' She rubbed the end of Percy's snout with a trembling hand. 'If I'd given it a thought, I'd have asked you to mention that my little dog needs help. He's very poorly.'

'I'll remember him when I'm Getting Through next.'

Roweena involuntarily pressed Percy closer, convinced that due to Lily's meddling she would hear her dog was to be taken from her. Was that the warning? Percy was to be stowed under the earth in her sunless cemetery, along with the dead pets of earlier years. She fought an urge to order Lily from her house, determined to regain peace of mind by any means.

Percy uttered a small whine. Crescents of white showed in each eye. His nose was like a dried prune.

Deeply humble, Lily said, 'I'll put up a petition for the little soul when we're next In Touch.' She was kneading her fingers together.

'What was this warning you were given? Tell me the message. You fill me with unease.' Roweena sat down near the stove.

'I felt you ought to know, not wait till tomorrow. This Presence gave a description. It was of something unusual happening, and my husband took it down.' She produced a slip of paper.

'Please read it. Then we'll have a cup of tea.' Roweena picked at the chipped enamel of her kettle, trying to charm away the horrid time impending.

'We began taking notes after our Friend had said it was for you. My husband wrote, 'The man puts his face against hers. Bitter taste in her mouth. Tears never to be wept.' Lily Falange

161

drew breath. 'The man sits by her, leans to kiss her. Removes his shoes. It is dark. She keeps very still.'

Roweena watched Lily's hands which held the scrap of paper. Percy's muzzle was flickering. He appeared to be asleep. "The man makes soft sounds. She thinks it is not her life." Roweena clutched Percy's blanket in a wild effort to comprehend. "The dark grows darker. She barely struggles. The man stands. She lies quiet, sleeping on her side. The man puts on his shoes and goes."

'Stop!' Roweena broke in, half-rising, the dog slipping precariously down her lap. 'Who was he talking about? Who is this person?' Visions of Octavia trapped . . . Octavia strangled on a bed. Speculating wildly, Roweena said, 'I'm going to London to see my daughter. You have given me the worst fright of my life. If there's no truth in it . . .'

'We'll all be very relieved, I'm sure,' Lily said sanctimoniously.

'Please look after Percy.' Roweena thrust him at her visitor and went to the door. 'Be kind to him, he's . . . he's very precious to me.' She went upstairs to find her bag, to stuff her purse inside and find a coat. Then, calling instructions to Lily to lock the house, she made for the garage.

Reversing with the roar of a giant mowing machine, Roweena swung round and accelerated towards the gate. She hooted at the bottom of the lane to dispense with halting, turned as tightly as the old car could manage, and shot uphill towards Brighton.

Dusk had fallen swiftly. She flustered for her lights, blank in the heat of the moment. She seldom drove at night now, and progressed in semi-obscurity for more than a hundred yards. As her lamps flared to cover the narrow road, its steep banks and curling corners, Roweena thought, What has Hugo done to us? Then jealous antipathy towards Hugo was displaced by a recurring bitterness against herself. How have I failed my daughter? Have I been terribly remiss? I should have been firmer with her, closer to her, tougher with myself . . .

The Morris panted and lusted up a yet steeper slope as if consuming the road that led to the Devil's Dyke. Were Hugo and Octavia in love? Roweena changed gear atrociously. And just then, from the shadow-laden verge some distance ahead, a figure emerged with arm outstretched.

In her preoccupied state, Roweena twitched the car over by

instinct. The man, advancing with a purposeful air, began to pump both his arms up and down. Roweena, whose only aim was to reach Brighton station and thence Octavia, in the least possible time, took the man to be a means to this end. Perhaps he had a message?

She braked sharply, skidding along the road. The engine stalled.

The man came slowly to the door. Roweena peered through her window to form an idea of him. Young or old? He appeared to have a leather jacket and a bag over his shoulder. Restarting the engine, Roweena shouted above the cacophony, 'Do you want a lift?'

Already he had wrenched the rear door open and was sliding inside. The engine stalled again. Roweena, exasperated by what now seemed a monstrous irrelevance in her crisis, revived the engine, engaged gear and lurched on. Her passenger hadn't said a word.

I'm a fool, Roweena told herself. Why should I help this man? I should put my daughter first. 'Where are you wanting to go?' she demanded. As she spoke, the memory flashed into her mind of a tale Lily Falange had told of a man who, travelling late along a main road, was signaled by a hitch-hiker to whom he gave a lift. It was a young woman and she climbed on to the back seat without a word. Asking a second time for her destination, the driver turned his head to find the girl had vanished.

What if my passenger is a ghost of the road? Roweena thought. Or a temporarily embodied spirit? Could this be part of an abominable trick devised by Lily?

'Where do you wish to be taken?' she demanded again, her voice rising.

She heard shuffling behind her, and the sound of his breathing. Undeniably he was man, not spirit. She could feel him lean over the back of her seat. She was on the point of explaining the urgent nature of her trip – it might have been helpful to relate the details to her passenger – when suddenly the man spoke. He said with rough humour, 'Anywhere will do for me.'

Roweena's concern for Octavia slid away, dwindled to a problem for the future. And all her wits, her prayers, were centred on the moment.